TELEPATHY OF GARDENS

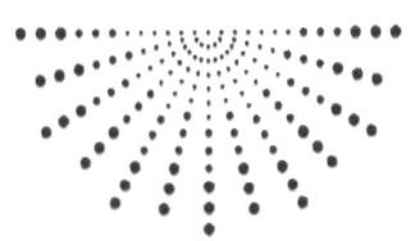

TELEPATHY OF GARDENS

REG RAWLINS, PSYCHIC INVESTIGATOR #5

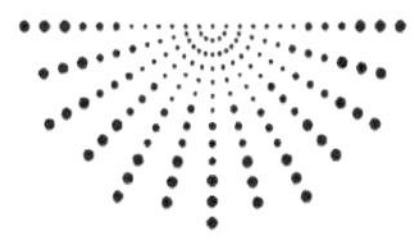

P.D. WORKMAN

ISBN: 9781989415382 (IS Hardcover)

ISBN: 9781989415375 (IS Paperback)

ISBN: 9781989415344 (KDP Paperback)

ISBN: 9781989415351 (Kindle)

ISBN: 9781989415368 (ePub)

pdworkman

Vegan Baked Alaska

Muffins Masks Murder

Tai Chi and Chai Tea

Santa Shortbread

Cold as Ice Cream

Changing Fortune Cookies

Hot on the Trail Mix

Recipes from Auntie Clem's Bakery

Zachary Goldman Mysteries

She Wore Mourning

His Hands Were Quiet

She Was Dying Anyway

He Was Walking Alone

They Thought He was Safe

He Was Not There

Her Work Was Everything

She Told a Lie

He Never Forgot

She Was At Risk

Kenzie Kirsch Medical Thrillers

Unlawful Harvest

Doctored Death (Coming soon)

Dosed to Death (Coming soon)

Gentle Angel (Coming soon)

AND MORE AT PDWORKMAN.COM

To those whose voices are not heard

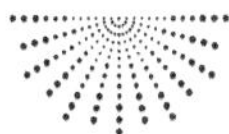

The kittens really were the cutest visitors Reg had ever had in the cottage. Nine pure-black little cats, they were almost impossible to tell apart. Yet they were each starting to show distinct personalities so that Reg could, in fact, tell one from the other. It was hard to believe that only days before, they had been draugrs, undead creatures raised by the Witch Doctor to do his bidding. Now, no one would guess that they had started their existence as zombies.

Francesca laughed as one little fellow chased her shoelace, so intent on it that Reg would have thought it really was a mouse or whatever kind of prey the cat imagined in his little kitty brain. "Come here, little kattakyn," blond-haired Francesca crooned in her Haitian Creole accent, "did you not hear Nicole tell you it was time to go bed? You are getting yourself all wound up instead of ready for sleep."

He continued to romp around her, pouncing on her shoelace and then darting back in retreat. Nearby, the kittens' surrogate mother, Nicole, patiently caught another of the kittens by the neck and wrestled it over to the pile where the others were washing or sleeping. They were too big for her to be bossing around, almost three-quarters her size, but she seemed determined that the little black cats were her own kittens and she would train them to obey her. She licked him and pressed him into place with the others, then approached the kitten that was playing with Francesca, making low meows and purrs as she called to him. He continued to jump at Francesca's shoelace and then retreat as if it were a dangerous snake.

"You are never going to get this one settled down," Francesca warned.

But Nicole was undaunted. She put one long foreleg over the kitten's shoulders, pinning him down, and then dug her teeth into the scruff of his neck to drag him over to the other kittens. While they were acting sleepy and getting ready for their naps, the last kitten was having nothing to do with it. He pounced on the nearest tail, then bit it, rousing one of the others. Nicole again pinned him with a foreleg, and then lay atop him, licking him soundly, forcing him to be still as she gave him a bath. The kitten wriggled and turned his head, but she kept a firm hold on him, all the while licking persistently until his eyes started to shut into slits and they were both purring in unison.

Reg shook her head, her thin red braids swinging around her face. "Well, I never would have thought she could do it. That little guy has ADHD if any kitten ever did. Always distracted by the nearest movement."

"Or shoelace," Francesca laughed.

"Well, you have to admit, it did look pretty lively."

Francesca shook her head, her tinkling laugh filling the room.

Reg felt relaxed and comfortable. She liked the aura that Francesca brought with her. Despite the logistics of bringing ten cats over to the cottage for a visit, Francesca never seemed to be frazzled. Nicole and the kittens themselves also brought a calming, happy presence into the house, like the warmth of a fire. After all of the dread and fear that Reg had suffered as the Witch Doctor raised his draugr army, Reg needed the beneficial feelings they brought.

Starlight was the only one who didn't seem happy with the

arrangements. It was understandable; the tuxedo cat with the mismatched eyes had been pining over Nicole since she had first appeared in the garden. Now that she was back inside and coming over for visits, she should have had plenty of time for him. But Nicole had been smitten with the kittens as soon as she had seen them and seemed oblivious to Starlight's advances.

"Don't you worry," Reg told Starlight, patting the seat of the upholstered couch beside her to invite him over. "The kittens will not be around forever. We need to find them all new homes. Then Nicole will have time for you."

He glared at her and washed his face, blaming her for the arrival of the furry interlopers.

It wasn't Reg's fault that the Witch Doctor had decided to make Black Sands his center of operations, nor that Francesca had charmed the draugrs into their kattakyn form and magically bound the Witch Doctor's life force that was dwelling within them. Reg hadn't wanted anything to do with the dark force from her past. She had been dragged into it by Corvin, much like the kittens being dragged by the scruff of their necks by Nicole.

It wasn't Reg's fault that she'd been recruited to protect Black Sands against zombies.

"We do need to find them new homes," Francesca agreed, watching the pile of black cats snoozing peacefully, Nicole on top of the pile looking very satisfied with herself. "It is vital that they are separated so that no one can unbind them. As long as they are kept apart from one another, Samyr Destine will not be able to re-form, and the world will be safe from him."

"Hard to believe that those little cats are all that separate Black Sands from the Witch Doctor's evil powers." Reg couldn't sense even a hint of the evil and dread that had accompanied the Witch Doctor. His force was completely suppressed by Francesca's spell. She and Corvin Hunter were the ones Black Sands owed their safety to. Without their powers, Reg and the others would easily have been killed, and the Witch Doctor would have gone on acquiring magical artifacts, gaining in strength, and raising more draugrs to do his bidding. Anyone who crossed his path or dared to stand up to him would be killed. It was a simple matter for a draugr to enter into its victim's dreams and to sit on his chest until he suffocated. Reg had only been spared that fate by Starlight's intervention. Reg wasn't sure how a real cat could fight off a dream cat that could kill despite not having real substance—but he had. The kattakyns were no longer dangerous, and it was easy to forget their origin, imagining instead that they were Nicole's natural kittens.

"How exactly are we going to find them homes all around the world?" Reg asked. "Is there some magical network that adopts cats?"

"These are very special cats," Nicole pointed out. "They will make good familiars. Even though the power of the bokor is bound, it is still there, and it will help to magnify the powers of the witch or warlock they are joined to."

"So is that a yes?"

"There is no magical network for cats," Francesca said, "but there are many people who will be happy to take one of these special cats. It is just a matter of finding the right homes. Not every cat is a good match for every practitioner."

Reg thought back to the day she had gone to the animal shelter and picked out Starlight. None of the other cats had responded to her the same way as Starlight. She knew that he was the cat she was supposed to have. The shelter worker's story of how Starlight had recently lost his old master and had not responded to anyone else who had approached him had sealed the deal. Reg needed a cat and he needed her. She hadn't anticipated just how compatible they would be. With the white star in the center of his forehead—his 'third eye,' as Sarah referred to it—his psychic powers were considerable. She was often surprised by how much he could boost her and enhance her psychic abilities when she needed a little extra help.

And he was furry and cute and lovely to cuddle up with when she was alone.

* * *

Starlight stopped washing and looked toward the window, his ears pricked forward.

"Someone out there?" Reg asked. Focusing her attention in the direction Starlight's ears pointed, she could sense Sarah Bishop, her landlord, along with someone else she wasn't familiar with. Sarah didn't seem to be headed toward Reg's door, so she wasn't bringing over a client or someone she wanted to introduce Reg to. Reg leaned over and pushed the curtain back an inch to see the two figures headed toward the garden. She only caught a glimpse of Sarah and the short man who was walking with her. Her seemingly middle-aged landlord was dressed in pink pants and a white shirt, with lots of pearls as accessories.

"Who is there?" Francesca asked.

"Sarah. Somebody else, maybe the new gardener."

"Good," Francesca approved. "That poor garden needs someone to take care of it."

Sarah had thrashed the garden with a broom when trying to shoo Nicole, then an unknown stray cat, out of the yard. The devastation caused by her impulsive act—the result of dementia caused by rapid aging—was significant. When Sarah had regained her health, she had attempted to rehabilitate the battered garden herself, but it was too much for her.

"Do you think I should go out and say hello?" Reg ventured, unsure what the proper etiquette was in a small town. She was only a tenant; Sarah was in charge of the yard and its upkeep, so it really wasn't any of her business.

Francesca shrugged. "You might introduce yourself. He is going to be working in your yard; it could be awkward if you keep walking by without saying anything."

"Okay. Makes sense," Reg agreed.

She got up and made her way to the garden back behind the house. Sarah was standing with the man, pointing out this and that. Reg wondered, looking at her newly-youthened face, whether she had also lost some weight with her transformation.

The gardener was quite short, probably suffering from some form of dwarfism. He was an old man with a wrinkled face and white beard. He had on green coveralls and a red cap. Reg couldn't avoid feeling his pain as he looked over the ruined garden.

Sarah turned, hearing Reg's approach. "Oh, Reg. Come and meet the gardener who is going to get my poor little garden back into shape again." She stretched her hand out in welcome and motioned toward the little man. "This is Mr. Blumenthal."

"Forst," the gardener introduced himself gruffly, holding out a calloused, stained hand.

Reg shook. He had a very strong grip—someone who had spent a lifetime working with his hands.

"I'm Reg Rawlins. I'm sorry this is such a mess." She gestured to the garden. She wasn't taking responsibility for the damage, of course, just acknowledging his pain at finding the plants in such poor condition. He cared very deeply about his work.

Forst gave a single nod. He looked back at Sarah for further instructions.

"Anyway," Sarah shrugged. "This is your area of expertise, so I don't have to tell you what needs to be done. Let me know if you can't find something you need. Come in for a cup of tea whenever you want one and have a break."

Reg was a little surprised that she was inviting a stranger into her house, especially with all of the trouble that a magical intruder could cause. But maybe Sarah had known him for a long time. Or maybe she had special wards or knew something about his magic or lack of it. It wasn't Reg's place to object. But she wouldn't be inviting him into her cottage.

"Nice to meet you," Reg told Forst. "Thank you for helping Sarah to get this fixed up. I know she'll be much happier once it is looking better again."

He gave another nod and said nothing.

Sarah walked Reg back to the cottage door. "Let me know if

you have any concerns," she said. "I don't want you to be disturbed by his work. If he is using a chainsaw during a seance… just let me know, and I'll take care of it."

"I'm sure it will be fine." As far as Reg could tell, there was no reason for Forst to be using any power tools. Sarah had beaten down the flowers and plants with a broom; it wasn't like Forst would need to cut down trees, and certainly not at midnight. He would be cleaning up the bits that were dead and maybe staking the plants that were bent over until they were strong enough to stand on their own again. But then, what did she know about gardening? The full extent of her plant-growing experience was planting beans for early school experiments. She'd never owned a houseplant, let alone tended a garden.

"He seems like a nice man," she told Sarah neutrally.

"They do tend to be very… laconic. Talk with each other, but not to outsiders."

"Outsiders?"

"Well, we aren't exactly his kind, are we?"

Reg came to a stop on her doorstep. "What exactly is his kind? Is he a fairy? A dwarf?"

Sarah laughed. "Fairies do have an affinity to nature and plants," she admitted, "but they are not likely to tend your garden for you. They are much too proud for that. They don't work for humans. And dwarves… you won't see them this near open waters. You're not likely to run into any dwarves outside the mountains, even in these modern times."

"Then what is he?"

"A gnome, dear." Sarah laughed again. "A garden gnome."

Reg had seen fake gnome statues in gardens, but she had no idea that they were really a thing. She shook her head at Sarah. "A garden gnome?"

"Of course. Who else would you get to rehabilitate a garden? A gnome will do it faster and with much better results than any other kind of expert. Those human landscapers that you can hire… well, they would take months to get my garden back to its natural glory. I would never hire a human to do a gnome's work."

"Of course not," Reg agreed dryly. "Who would do that?"

"Exactly," Sarah agreed. "Well, I shall leave you to your guest." A crease between her eyebrows, Sarah glanced at the living room window where Starlight was poking his head out between the curtains waiting for Reg's return. Reg wondered whether she could sense the other cats. Sarah would not have been happy to find so many cats in the cottage. She tolerated Starlight as Reg's familiar but had blanched at even the thought of a second cat around when Reg had started to look for Nicole.

Sarah had an African gray parrot and an affinity for birds, and she did not like cats.

* * *

Reg sat down again with Francesca. She looked at the cats all snoozing in a pile and picked up Starlight to give him some attention while she talked.

"So what do you need me for?" she asked Francesca. "It seems like you've got a pretty good handle on the market for the kattakyns. I don't know anything about giving cats away. I always wanted a cat as a kid, and I tried bringing abandoned kittens or stray cats home more than once, but that never worked out. Foster moms are usually overworked as it is, they don't need another mouth to feed or critter to look after. Even if I promised to take care of all of its needs, I could never convince anyone to let me have one. So I'm not sure how much help I would be to your case."

Francesca smiled, watching Reg pet Starlight, scratch his ears, and rub the white spot on his forehead. "It is not your marketing expertise that I am hoping for," she said with a lilt. "I am looking for someone who can help to match the kattakyns with the right owners. The ones who will suit them the best."

"Oh." Reg thought once more to her tour of the animal shelter, eventually finding Starlight there. She had found the cat that suited her the best or needed her the most, but was that a transferable skill? "I don't know. I've never done anything like that before."

"You are very good with the kittens," Francesca pointed out. "You can see their personalities. You can tell them apart."

"Well, yes, that's true. But they do have very distinct personalities; you've noticed that too, right?"

Francesca shook her head. She adjusted the lay of her sweater, looking uncomfortable. "No, I am afraid not… as much as I try, I only see nine little black cats. We want to be able to match them up with the practitioners who best suit them."

"Okay. Well, I guess I'll do my best."

"You want them to be happy in their new homes. We need them to stay put, not to roam around and find each other."

"Do you think that would happen? It wouldn't, would it? They would get lost, but they wouldn't be able to find each other. They wouldn't know where to go."

"They are bound together. They will eventually find each other. We want to keep that from happening for as long as possible. By placing them around the world, I hope to keep them apart for hundreds of years. The farther they are apart, the less chance there is of Samyr gathering enough power to reform himself."

Reg shuddered. "Okay, I'm in," she agreed.

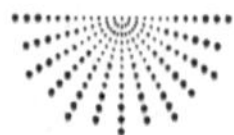

*R*eg helped Francesca carry the cats to her car in a couple of boxes. Since they were half-grown rather than small kittens, they couldn't all be corralled in a shoebox. They scrabbled around in the large boxes, their claws slipping on the slick cardboard. A couple of them started meowing, protesting their situation. They put the boxes on the back seat of the car. Reg smiled at all of the inquisitive black furry faces looking back at her. She pushed a couple down when they tried to climb up out of the boxes and sent them calm, reassuring thoughts. Eventually, they all settled.

Francesca nodded and got into the driver's seat. "Thank you, Reg! I will be in touch when I have had a chance to talk to some of the potential buyers. Then we can sort out which one to send where."

"Okay. Sounds good. Drive slow."

"I do not want to have any accidents with this cargo," Francesca agreed, taking a look over her shoulder at them.

After Francesca's car pulled out, Reg became aware she was being watched. She looked around and saw a white compact car. Not a surprise, since the town was full of white compacts, but she knew by the feeling that started to grow and thicken around her precisely who it was.

Corvin extricated himself from the small car and approached her. His handsome face was sullen. "I've been waiting half the day for you to get rid of that woman and her cats."

"Oh?" Reg gave a careless shrug. That was another bonus of a houseful of cats—it kept Corvin at a distance. "I don't remember you calling or mentioning that you wanted to come over."

He looked like he had tasted something sour. "That would probably be because you've blocked me on your phone."

Reg smiled. "Yeah, that's probably it."

"But I still know where you live. All that means is that I have to come over here in person, which is not exactly a hardship. I would rather see you face to face."

That was a drawback of cutting off phone communications. Reg would have to rethink that. It wasn't like she could get a restraining order to keep him from hanging around her house. He wasn't doing anything to threaten or harm her. Reg also had no desire to stand before a judge and plead her case. She made it a policy to stay as far as possible from police and courtrooms.

Corvin's eyes roamed around. "Why don't we go for a walk?"

He knew, of course, that she wouldn't allow him in her house. Not with his track record. It was dangerous to invite any unknown warlock into the house. All that much worse, one like Corvin whose dangers were known.

"I'm not going for a walk with you. Spit out what it is you want because I'm going back to my house and you're not going to stop me."

"There's no need to be so vehement about it."

"There is every reason."

"I just wanted to talk. You know I don't have very many options of who to talk to right now."

"It's not my fault you are being shunned."

"Well…" He raised his brows. "It is sort of your fault."

"You're the one who attacked me. If you mean it's my fault

because I testified against you, then fine. It's my fault you're being shunned."

He didn't look pleased that she had agreed with him. He was looking for a fight. Looking to engage with her. Reg couldn't afford to let him work his wiles on her. She looked at her phone to see what time it was.

"So, what did you want to talk about? Do you actually have a purpose here, or are you just hanging around because you're bored?"

He took a step closer to her, into her comfort zone. Reg took a step back and tried to raise her psychic defenses against him. Sooner or later, he would make his move. She needed to be ready for it. He wouldn't be able to resist trying to magic her.

"I didn't say I was bored," Corvin said, staring into her eyes, his manner confidential and intense.

"Well, good. Then I guess you have plenty to do and don't need to bother me."

"Regina," he crooned her name, correctly pronouncing it, Reh JEE nah, not like the Canadian city. "When are you going to stop this dance? Just admit that the two of us are fated. Stop fighting every word and every move. I don't want to hurt you. I want us to be friends."

"You want a lot more than friendship, and I'm not going to give it to you."

He shifted his feet, looking for a more comfortable position. But he wasn't going to her cottage, they weren't going for a walk, and he was too far away from his car to lean casually against it. He could only stand there, out in the open where everyone could see him, talking with Reg. Because that was all she was going to let him do. As handsome as the dark warlock was, and however enticing he could become when he exercised his charms, she couldn't give in.

Corvin leaned closer. "You realize that things could change very quickly."

She didn't like his proximity. Was he making a threat? Having gained so much more power in his fight with the Witch Doctor, who knew what he could do now. Or was he suggesting something else?

"What things could change?" she asked cautiously.

"The Council is considering commuting my sentence."

Reg felt like she had been punched in the gut. After all of the pain and suffering she had gone through, after having to face the humiliation of testifying against him, they were going to let him get off that quickly? They had said that they would shun him until he proved he could be a positive member of their society. His sentence was indefinite, and Reg had thought that meant it would be long, not short.

"How can they do that?" she asked breathlessly.

"Our encounter with the Witch Doctor proved that I am a valuable asset to the magical community. We saved countless lives and bound a dark force that could have done unimaginable harm."

"You didn't exactly do it for altruistic purposes."

"Who is to say?" he countered with a smug smile. "When I tell the story to the Council members, it certainly will be."

"The only reason you went into that warehouse was so that you could have access to the magical artifacts and consume their powers."

"Not the only reason."

"And to prove that you could defeat a powerful being. An immortal, or whatever he was."

Corvin's smile just grew. Reg shook her head, sickened by his attitude and the thought that the warlock council might reinstate him so quickly. It was beyond belief. How had he been punished for what he had tried to do to her? He had gone against all of the rules imposed on his kind and tried to steal her powers from her by force. If they reinstated him so quickly, it would be a sign that they didn't care what he did. He could go on doing whatever he liked; they didn't care a bit about his victims.

"Reg…" He cocked his head, looking at her like she had hurt

him by not being excited about his news. He made a pouty face. "Don't be that way. I don't harbor ill will toward you. We can be friends. Forget the past, and look forward to the future."

"To a future where you can have whatever you want because you're the strongest? Where you can break all of the rules and no one cares about it one bit?"

"Obviously, people care, or they wouldn't have disciplined me to begin with. But I've learned my lesson. I won't let my appetites get away from me again." He blinked and smiled encouragingly. "You and I can get along. Our powers are synergistic. They go together so well, matching each other strength for strength. The two of us together could defeat any foe."

"Oh, that's your new line, is it? Now that you've got the power, you're ready to use it. And it's not to protect all of the innocent citizens of Black Sands anymore. Now it is to defeat all foes and get what you want."

"That isn't what I said. Think of how many people could benefit if you and I combined our powers. Think of all of those people that you would like to be able to help. The two of us together could do almost anything. Think about all of your lost and broken dreams. All of those things that you used to want that you've given up on. You could have them all."

Reg shook her head, trying to rid herself of his influence, like a fly buzzing in her ear. He didn't understand anything about her childhood and her lost and broken dreams. He thought that she had dreamed of money and power. But in reality, she had dreamed of a loving family, stability, enough to eat, and a future. She was doing well in Black Sands, but it was only a matter of time until that dream ended too. They would come for her and she would have to run again if she wanted to avoid incarceration. She would be on the skids once more, looking for a home and a stable income somewhere else where people had never heard her name.

"Reg." He reached out to touch her cheek. "You look so sad. You can have anything. Think about it. Whatever you want."

She could feel his warmth even before his fingers touched her skin. She swallowed and closed her eyes, wishing that she could swim into the warm, safe feeling that he promised. But she knew how she would feel if she surrendered to him. When he was done with her and had stripped away all of her gifts, she would be left an empty husk, with a hollow, echoing space in her head that used to be filled with voices. She would be more alone than she had ever been before. She pulled back from his touch, forcing herself to withdraw instead of leaning into him.

"Corvin…" She rarely addressed him by name, rarely told him anything about her past or how she was feeling. "You have no idea what it's like for me."

She opened her eyes and looked at him. Corvin frowned, wrinkle lines forming between his eyes. He pulled back his hand. "Then tell me. I know what it's like to hold those powers. I don't know how you could be unhappy with the richness of the powers in your possession." It was his turn to look at her longingly. He had untold powers after consuming many of the magical artifacts at the warehouse and the powers of the Witch Doctor himself. Anyone else would have been satisfied with that. But not Corvin. He had to have it all. He had to have Reg's powers too.

"How could you still be hungry?"

He shrugged and chuckled. "You know how you can spend a couple of hours eating at a buffet, until you're absolutely stuffed, and still want the dessert afterward?"

"And I'm your dessert?"

"Well, not you, but your powers."

"It's the same thing. I don't want to be consumed. You don't know what it feels like."

"Oh, but I do," Corvin reminded her. He had told them all at his hearing how his father, also a power-drinker like him, had consumed his powers multiple times. Because Corvin could gain power from other people and magical objects, then unlike most of the practitioners in existence, he could have his powers stripped away more than once. Reg looked away from him, embarrassed to remember his vulnerability.

"If you know what it's like, then how can you do it to someone else?" she demanded. "How can you do that, knowing how empty they will feel after you take their powers?"

"Because I need to do it to survive. Do you like the fact that animals are killed for your consumption? That to survive, you kill other living creatures?"

"Well… I don't like to think about it, no. But it isn't like I'm killing them myself. And if it weren't for the agricultural industry, I wouldn't eat them at all. It's just because… they are there. If I stopped eating animals, it wouldn't change anything in the industry."

"So if you won't stop killing other creatures to fill your appetites, then why would you criticize me for doing what comes naturally for me? I need to consume others' powers for my survival."

"I could decide to be vegetarian; then I wouldn't be eating animals. You could choose to just consume the powers from objects, not from people."

"Think of the pain you would be inflicting on the plants you ate. Is that any better than killing animals? You consume them alive!"

"Plants don't have feelings!" Reg rolled her eyes.

"Tell that to a nature guardian. Those who tend to the plants know better."

Reg shifted uncomfortably. She looked at him, squirming. "You don't need my powers right now. You don't need anyone's powers right now. You're still full from the buffet. With the amount that you filled up before the Witch Doctor gave up, you shouldn't need to feed again for about a century."

"You don't know anything about how long it will last," Corvin pointed out grumpily.

"I know that you're full right now."

"And did I say I was going to consume your powers? I suggested that the two of us could work together. That's all."

"And that you would still like dessert."

"A man always wants dessert."

"I'm going inside. I really don't want to talk about this anymore. I'm not about to become Bonnie to your Clyde, so you can forget about that. You're on your own."

He mouthed the words, Bonnie and Clyde, like he had no idea what she was talking about. The magical world could be so isolated from the real world. They just lived in their own little pockets, ignoring the rest of the world. Some of them didn't have any electronics. No phones. No TVs. Reg had no idea how they could survive without modern conveniences. It was a modern world.

"The answer is no, Corvin. I'm not teaming up with you. I wasn't happy about being forced to team up with you against the Witch Doctor. I'm done."

Corvin blew out his breath, frustrated. "You owe me. You just remember that. We are bonded together until you repay me your part of the covenant."

Reg swallowed. "You took my powers. The contract was fulfilled."

"I returned them to you. That means you still owe me. You agreed. You made a covenant. And until you fulfill it, we will be fated to cross paths."

"Ick. I'm going home. You can sit in your car and wait for me to come out again. Or you could go home and do whatever warlocky things are on your magical to-do list."

Reg pulled back, forcing herself to leave his circle of influence. The cooler air caressed her skin and she was able to take a full breath again. She had failed to notice just how much he had been stifling her.

She went back to her cottage, looking back once or twice to make sure that Corvin wasn't following her. He stayed out in front of the main house.

CHAPTER THREE

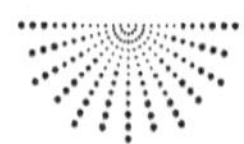

She was tired when she got back indoors. It had taken a lot of energy to fight the temptation to join Corvin. Even though he hadn't been magicking her the same way as he had in the past, he had still been doing something. Maybe he was trying out a new power. A way of influencing her with different methods from those he had used before. Who knew what powers he had acquired from the artifacts in the warehouse and the Witch Doctor?

Starlight meowed at Reg, scolding her for going away for so long. Or maybe he could smell Corvin's scent on her or sense that she had been talking to him. She hadn't actually been outside for that long. She stooped down and picked him up.

"I know, I know, Star. I didn't know he was coming over, and I didn't let him ensorcell me, so everything is fine."

He purred and rubbed the velvety top of his head against her chin. He reminded her that *he* was her cat. Not Nicole, and not the nine kattakyns. He was the one who had chosen her, and she was marked as his territory. She was his human.

"You're a silly cat, you know?" Reg said. "You think that you're the owner and I'm your pet when it's the other way around."

His disdainful gaze clearly communicated that she had it backward.

* * *

Reg was awake early the next morning, despite having been up for a midnight seance. For some reason, when the sun started to creep in through her window, she was wide awake. She made her morning coffee and gave Starlight some stew from the fridge to supplement his dry cat food, and was looking on her phone for a morning show that she had watched a few times before. Usually, she wasn't up early enough to see it. But it was easier for her to keep up on the news through televised programs than by reading articles.

As she stood next to the coffee pot, waiting for it to finish dripping, she heard crying. A man's voice, sobbing, "Oh, no, no, no…"

She looked at her phone at first, thinking that it was a pop-up commercial she had failed to dismiss. But it wasn't her phone. She hit the mute button on the morning show to silence their animated, chattering voices so she could hear where the sound was coming from. While it seemed much closer, she finally determined that it was coming from outside. She looked out her windows that faced the garden, but still couldn't see what was going on, so she went outside for a peek.

Forst, the garden gnome, was sitting on a big rock, his face in his hands, weeping loudly. Reg stood looking at him, unsure what to do. It was a private moment, and she was sure he wouldn't want to be interrupted or have to explain his sorrow to her. She should go back into the cottage and mind her own business.

But she couldn't get past his heartbroken sobs. She couldn't just leave him there to deal with whatever had made him so unhappy without at least offering a listening ear. What good was a psychic who wouldn't listen?

"Uh… Mr. Blumenthal…?"

He raised his head and looked at her. He started immediately to his feet as if she'd caught him doing something forbidden.

"Miss Rawlins!"

His blue eyes were watery and red, but his face was otherwise an unreadable mask. If she hadn't caught him crying, she wouldn't have been able to read his sorrow in the lines of his face. She took a couple of steps closer.

"I'm sorry. I didn't mean to startle you. It's just that... you sounded so sad. I wanted to make sure that everything is okay. Are you... all right?"

He rubbed at his nose with the back of his hand and reached into the pocket of his coveralls. He drew out a strange, curvy pipe like Reg had seen on Sherlock Holmes movie covers, and started to fiddle with it, filling it and lighting it without looking at her. His hands shook slightly, but otherwise, he betrayed no emotion.

But in her head, Reg again heard the sobs. "She's just a girl. What could she do?"

His lips hadn't moved and he continued to focus on his pipe, drawing in a long drag of smoke and then puffing it out in rings. Reg suddenly realized that she hadn't heard him with her natural ears, but had been hearing his thoughts. She looked away, embarrassed. It wasn't polite to listen in on other people's private thoughts. She hadn't meant to enter his head and wasn't sure how she had.

"I'll help you if there is anything I can do," she offered. She looked up at the pale blue sky. There were white clouds toward the horizon, but overhead it was just blue sky, a few birds far above them.

"A human does not help a gnome. But it is the humans we must deal with."

Reg waited. She made an offering gesture with her hands, not sure what else to say to him. He squinted at her, his blue eyes taking on a new expression.

"You hear my words?"

Reg nodded. "Yes. I'm sorry, I wasn't trying to read your

thoughts. I don't know what happened. Maybe I'm extra-sensitive after the seance last night," she explained, aware that she was saying too much, providing information he didn't need.

"Humans cannot hear inside words."

"No. Not usually. But I'm a psychic. So I guess… I can. I'm sorry. I didn't mean to intrude."

He pulled the pipe away from his mouth, giving a sudden smile. His cheeks were red and his eyes brighter.

"Talking with humans is usually so hard."

She remembered his curtness when they had been introduced the day before. Maybe he hadn't been rude or abrupt, but just had problems forming words aloud.

"Do gnomes talk to each other… with their inside words?" she guessed.

He nodded vigorously. "That is our way," he agreed. "The outside words… are much harder."

"Well, you can talk to me with your inside words. I didn't mean to overhear you, but if there's something I can do to help, I would be happy to."

He puffed on his pipe again and considered. Reg realized she couldn't hear all of his private thoughts, only the words he wished to share, and was relieved. Maybe she hadn't been as rude as she had feared.

"It is my brother," he told her finally. "Fir, my twin."

"You have a twin?"

"All gnomen have a twin."

"Really? I didn't know that. That must be really… nice. You would always have someone to talk to, growing up. Someone who was always there for you." The loneliness of her childhood had been a far different story. Reg had moved from family to family, never with anyone who could understand her thoughts and feelings, who understood her past and could be empathetic toward her. She had longed for a sister she could share her thoughts with. There had been the occasional foster sister she had connected with, like Erin, but it had mostly been a lonely existence.

Forst nodded his head. "Gnomen twins rely on each other. We are closely bound."

That made sense to Reg. She'd always thought that twins must be the closest kind of relationship there was. In contact with each other from the time they were conceived, spending time together in the womb communing with each other and becoming familiar with each other's patterns and feelings.

"And something happened to your twin? What is it?"

The gnome was still holding his pipe in his right hand; his left clenched into a fist. Reg felt his distress heighten.

"He has been captured! Locked in a cage!"

"Oh, dear." Reg looked around, hoping that Sarah might be walking by. She didn't understand a lot of things about the magical world, and if some evil witch or other creature had kidnapped Forst's brother, Reg was going to need help from someone with much deeper knowledge and experience. "Captured by who? What happened?"

"The black coats took him away. They said he could not protect his patch any longer. That he was doing wrong and had to be punished." Forst's hand unclenched and reclenched. He tried to keep a hold on himself, but could not restrain another desperate sob.

"Who are these black coats? Are they witches? Something else? Where did they take him?"

"To the cage, the cage!" he wailed. "How can they lock up a free creature?"

Reg couldn't help walking closer to the gnome, and hesitated, not knowing if she could touch him, or if that would be considered inappropriate or an assault. He looked up at her, his eyes swimming with tears.

"What did they say he did wrong?" Reg prompted.

"They want to destroy his patch. They want to kill the plants. Humans always want to destroy everything! He did nothing but protect his own living."

Reg caught on the thoughts she could understand. "It was humans who took him? What kind of humans?"

"The black coats," he repeated. "They took him away and put him in a cage."

Understanding was dawning on Reg. "Do you mean police? Black shirts and pants, with badges and shields on them?" Reg gestured to her own chest and shoulder.

Forst nodded miserably.

"He was arrested? What did they say they were arresting him for?"

"For protecting his plants."

"What kind of plants?" Reg asked suspiciously. "Did he have… special plants? Like marijuana?"

"No," Forst's brow wrinkled. "No ditch weed. Not plants humans care about. They want to kill them."

"Why?"

"Building roads. Houses. Replacing everything with stone. Why do humans like stone so much? They must be part dwarf."

"Development." Reg finally understood. "Where is his property? Are they going to pay him for it?"

"Gold," Forst shook his head grumpily. "You cannot kill plants for gold. Gnomen need living things, not metal and rocks."

"I'm sorry," Reg shook her head. "Humans can be big bullies."

Forst tugged on her sleeve, looking up at her pleadingly. "You will talk to the black coats?" he begged. "You will get him out of the cage?"

Reg sighed.

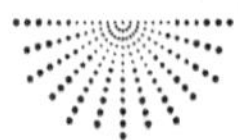

The last thing that Reg wanted to do was to talk to the police. Well, maybe the second last, the last being to be alone with Corvin Hunter. She didn't want to talk to them or to go to the police station or bail a gnome out of jail.

But she couldn't bear the abject misery on Forst's face. He didn't have a clue how the human justice system worked. He didn't know what to do and even if he did, his ability to speak—his outside words—were limited. He needed someone who knew what she was doing and could talk to the police to find out how to have his twin released.

She could call the main number for the police department, but she hoped to shortcut that by calling Detective Jessup, who could maybe smooth the way for her. Jessup could at least talk to the officers involved in the arrest, in case they were not part of the magical community. It didn't seem like very many in the police department knew about the magical community. Which must make some of the crime they dealt with in Black Sands seem very bizarre.

"Reg," Jessup greeted when she saw Reg's caller ID on the phone and picked up the call. She sounded pleased. It was back to 'Reg' instead of 'Miss Rawlins,' which she reverted to when Reg was a person of interest. "What can I do for you?"

This time she was interested in helping. Reg decided to use it to her best advantage.

"I have a friend with a problem."

"Sure. What's the problem?"

"His brother has been arrested; I'm not sure what for. Sounds like he got in the way of some developer who wants to appropriate his land. He's in jail, and…"

"And you want to know how to get him out."

"Yes. Maybe on bail, or maybe just to have the charges dropped. I doubt if he's really guilty of any lawbreaking."

"If he's been arrested, I have to assume that he did something. What's this guy's name?"

"Fir Blumenthal."

"Okay, hang on a second." Reg could hear her computer keys tapping away. "Ooh. Eco-terrorism?"

"Seriously? What the heck is eco-terrorism?"

"Looks like he is suspected of sabotaging a bunch of industrial equipment. Trespassing. He chained himself to a tree."

"He's just trying to protect his land."

"Doesn't work if it's not your own land. You know anything about the backstory?"

"Well… he's a gnome."

"Ah. We've run into this kind of thing before. They don't understand the way the modern world works. Private ownership of land and development and that kind of thing. They think that whatever land they squat on is theirs, and they'll buckle down and do whatever they can to keep other people from destroying 'their' land or removing them from it."

"Isn't there any treaty protecting them? Don't they have any of their own land? Any rights?"

"They've never been particularly interested in making agreements with humans or any other races. They just want to tend their gardens or forests and be left alone. Unfortunately… there's more and more encroachment on their land, and it's getting harder and harder for them to find virgin territory where they can stay for any amount of time."

"So what can you do? Can you get the charges dropped? Get him out on bail?"

"I can try talking to the powers that be around here. He probably hasn't given any explanation of why he was acting the way he was. They think he's just some eco-nut."

"And you can convince them otherwise?"

"I'll do my best. Are you going to come down here to get him?"

"Uh… I'd rather not. But if I have to."

"Could you? It helps to have some citizen saying that he's not a danger and he's not going to cause any more trouble. Because I doubt he'll defend himself. They aren't much for talking."

"Well, for outside talking."

There was a pause. "Outside talking?"

"That's what they call it—communicating out loud. Forst says it's really hard for them. But they're fine with inside talking."

"And what is inside talking?"

"Telepathy."

"Oh." Jessup laughed. "Trust you! The trouble is, they can't communicate telepathically with the rest of us. The cops aren't going to know how to communicate with him. He's not deaf or disabled. They can talk if forced to. So people assume that they're just hard to get along with."

"Can't you tell them he is disabled?"

"I'll try. It's not exactly true, but I can't very well tell them he's a gnome."

"What would you tell them if he could only speak using a voice synthesizer or picture board or sign language?"

"I wouldn't have any problem telling them that he was disabled then. Because it's true."

"Then how is this any different? He's not physically built for verbal communication. It doesn't matter if he can say a word here and there. He needs assistance. Accommodations."

"Well… yeah. So when you get down here, you can have a little chat with him in a private meeting room, and then you can advocate for him. I'm sure if you make a big stink about how his rights are being violated because of his disability, they'll be quick enough to let him go. No one wants that kind of publicity."

* * *

Reg took Jessup's advice and stormed into the police station, demanding that she be allowed to see her client, making plenty of noise about how they were brutalizing a homeless, disabled man, ripping him from his home and treating him like an animal, locking him up in a cage.

"Ma'am, ma'am," the desk clerk made motions for her to calm down. "Please, there's no need to yell. I don't know what has happened, but I'm sure we can work it out. Abusive language and behavior are not going to get you anywhere and will not be tolerated."

"You've locked him up! Don't you people have any sense? Aren't your officers given any disability training? But what was I expecting in a run-down little Podunk town like this? Of course you're going to act like commandos instead of knowing how we treat people in the twenty-first century."

"Who is it you are here to talk to us about?" the clerk asked, fingers hovering over the keyboard.

"Fir Blumenthal. Arrested yesterday afternoon. For daring to sit on his own property."

The woman brought the record up on her screen and scanned the information. "According to this, he was not sitting on his own property. He is not the registered owner, and the owner wanted him removed."

"Have you never heard of homelessness? Squatting? Just because someone doesn't have title, that doesn't mean they don't have rights! You can't just lock people up because they don't have a place to live! It's outrageous."

"I'm sure we can get this all sorted out. Do you have a place for Mr. Blumenthal to go? Someone who will vouch for him and put him up?"

"Now you're going to treat him like he's incompetent when you haven't even met him? Just because he has different communication needs than you, that doesn't make him less of a person. It doesn't mean he can't take care of himself. He has the same rights as anyone else. Do you require anyone else to prove that they'll be 'taken care of' when they are released?"

"I just meant... you said that he didn't have a home... I would be remiss if I didn't try to make sure that he was going to a safe situation and wasn't just going to be out on the street."

"Do you know how many homeless people there are out there? Are you telling me that the police are in the business of making sure that they all have safe homes to go to? That's not your job. You can't discriminate against him because he's indigent."

The clerk rolled her shoulders, frowning and trying to find some way to handle the situation without being ripped apart for being elitist or ableist. "Look, ma'am. I'm trying to help you here. This man was arrested for being a nuisance and a possible danger. We can't just let him go and pretend that nothing happened."

"Of course you can, you do it all the time. If there isn't enough evidence to build a case against Mr. Blumenthal, then you have to let him go. You can't just keep holding him because his brain doesn't work the same way as yours does. People who are considered to be a danger are released all the time. Suspected murderers, pedophiles, drug dealers. If you don't have enough to convict them, you have to let them go. End of story."

The clerk sighed, putting her hands flat on the desk in front of her and bowing her head in defeat. "Let me find someone who can help you with this."

* * *

Reg was shunted from one person to another, giving her spiel and attacking wherever possible, until someone agreed that she should be allowed to talk to her client. No one asked what kind of client he was. Probably no one dared, knowing she could go into a rant about how patients' rights were protected and they weren't allowed to ask anything that invaded his privacy or his relationship to a counselor or social worker or medical professional, whatever it was that Reg was pretending to be.

"Detective Jessup said that you were coming and that you would want to meet with Mr. Blumenthal," a tall, thin policeman advised Reg, acting like he had known what was going on all the time and hadn't been caught off-guard by Reg's invasion of the police department or Jessup's call advising that they should help her out. "If you'll just come this way…"

Reg followed the policeman. She couldn't help grinning when he wasn't looking at her. She'd never had so much fun in a police station, and she'd pulled some pretty bold scams in her time. She was enjoying the outraged mama bear act.

He offered her a seat on one of the plastic chairs, offered her coffee or water, and promised that Mr. Blumenthal would be brought in shortly. Reg sat down to relax, knowing that it could be another hour or more before they made it through all of the bureaucratic roadblocks and got him from the jail cell to the meeting room. She looked around the room, painted a flat green, with anti-drug posters, warnings about not smoking, and various other visual pollution.

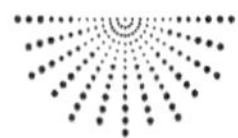

*E*ventually, Fir was brought into the meeting room. Reg could see at a glance that he had been poorly treated. Plenty of fodder for her outrage.

"Is this the way you treat all prisoners?" she demanded. "Or just the homeless and disabled ones?"

The tall police officer looked at her with apprehension. "I was not involved in his arrest. I don't know anything about the way that he's been treated."

"No?" Reg demanded. "You can't tell just by looking at him? His clothes are dirty and torn; he has a black eye and abrasions on his face—who knows about the rest of his body! Did the police beat him? Or did you just put him in with the general population where the other prisoners would abuse him? I will be calling the media, and this may just make the front page. Is that what you want to see? Mr. Blumenthal's battered face on the front page of the Black Sands paper? Maybe this is big enough it will make it to Miami, or even a national paper! This is outrageous."

"Ma'am, I think you need to calm down. Sit down and have a visit with your… friend. I'm sure you'll find that he's been treated with respect. If there have been any violations, we can address the specifics. Mr. Blumenthal has not had any complaints. He has not asked for a doctor or anything else."

She glared at him. "Mr. Blumenthal is nonverbal," she said acidly.

He swallowed, made a helpless gesture, and fled from the room, shutting the door behind him. Reg glanced around for surveillance equipment. There was no obvious camera or observation window. But that didn't mean that it was free of listening devices. She looked at Fir Blumenthal, sitting across the table from her, looking tiny and thoroughly baffled by what was going on. She leaned closer to him.

"Forst sent me," she said softly. "You can use your inside words and I will hear you."

His eyes widened. He looked very much like his brother. Of course, they were twins and the first gnomes she had ever encountered, so it was understandable that they would resemble each other. She didn't think they were identical twins, but Fir had the same white beard and round face as Forst. He had no cap, showing off a pale, gleaming scalp.

"You can hear us?"

"Yes. I can hear you. I came to help. Forst is very upset about you being arrested and wanted me to see what I could do about getting you out. I hope that my yelling doesn't bother you; it's just a way of getting the black coats to pay attention. They're not very good listeners."

"You can yell," Fir agreed, the corner of his mouth lifting in a small smile. "If that's what will free me from this cage."

Reg nodded. She looked at his injuries, the sadness that Forst had felt earlier washing over her. They had hurt the poor, defenseless little man just because he was different and vulnerable. He wanted to protect his plants from the developers who wanted to bulldoze them all away, and for that, they had hurt him and imprisoned him. "Tell me about what happened. Who hit you?"

Fir rubbed his abraded cheek, flinching slightly at his own touch. He touched his blackened, puffy eye tenderly. "Some of it from the black coats. The eyes and the worst pains, from the other humans in the cage." His large nostrils flared. "They call us animals, but animals do not behave that way. Only humans behave that way, attacking and imprisoning and causing harm."

"I know. We don't have a very good track record, do we?"

He again smiled, a little sunnier this time. "You are different. How did Forst know you could hear inside talk?"

"Well..." She didn't know if she should reveal that she had heard him weeping. Did the gnomes have a social code that men should not show emotion? Or would he think it was normal and appropriate? "I heard him... talking to himself. So I knew. I didn't even realize at first that it was inside talk and not outside talk; it was so clear in my head."

"You will be able to get me out of here?"

"I think so. I have a friend who is going to try to help. She's here in the police station, though I don't know exactly where right now."

"You can talk to her too?"

"I can talk to her. Telepathically, you mean? No. I just talked to her on the phone earlier. I'll have to wait until she comes here or calls me back. She can't understand telepathy."

He nodded. He picked at the dirt under his nails. His hands were calloused from plenty of manual labor. She pictured him working in his garden, tending to his plants.

He smiled at her. "Yes. I miss my garden."

"Where is it? Who is the developer that wants to ruin it?"

Fir described the location, and Reg, picturing it, tried to place it on her mental map. He talked about the plants that grew there and what each one liked as if they were his children. He spoke of the small stream that watered them and the water birds that came to drink and to hunt for insects.

"That sounds lovely. I can understand why you don't want to leave it."

"I must get back there." His eyes swam with tears. "I must get home to my living things."

Reg nodded. She looked toward the door, but Jessup didn't immediately appear. "Tell me about what you did before they came to get you. They said that you vandalized their property and that you were trespassing after they told you to leave."

He described the things he had done to their vehicles and heavy equipment, and Reg suppressed a smile. She couldn't help cheering for the underdog, the little man fighting the big corporation. She delighted in the things he had done to show the company that he wasn't going to be walked all over.

"You understand that they say the property is not yours? That it belongs to someone else and they want to change it?"

"They want to kill it. They want to kill all of the plants and put in their stone highway and monstrosities. Any soil that is left, they will cover with their carpets of tame grass, and they won't even let that grow properly. They will plant trees and a few foreign flowers and then pat themselves on the back that they have made it look 'natural.' How could such a monstrosity be natural?"

"How much space is in your patch? How big is it?"

He shrugged. "A garden gnome does not need much. But we are being squeezed out of even the tiniest plots. They want it to be all stone and shelters that block out the light. They want nothing that is wild to be left."

Reg nodded, thinking about it. There was a tap on the door, and Jessup put in an appearance, poking her head in first to make sure that it was safe to enter.

"Come in." Reg motioned to one of the other plastic chairs. "Unless you've already figured out how to get Mr. Blumenthal out of here and we don't have to wait any longer."

"No such luck," Jessup said with a grimace. "But the gears are turning. It's in the works. Hopefully…"

"As you can see, Mr. Blumenthal—"

"Fir," the gnome inserted.

"Fir has not been treated well while in police custody. He's been beaten up by the police who arrested him and by the other inmates in custody. Why they would think it was okay to put a defenseless, disabled man into the general population, I have no idea."

"I've already talked to them about it. Although I didn't know the condition he was in. You, I mean," Jessup said, facing the gnome and addressing him directly.

"What kind of human is she?" Fir asked Reg, studying the Asian woman curiously. He had apparently not had a lot of interaction with humans of different races.

Reg answered Fir in her head instead of out loud. "I don't know for sure. It isn't polite to ask."

"She is not very ugly for a human."

Reg snickered and didn't pass this information on to Jessup.

"So how long do you think it is going to take? Maybe we can get Mr.—Fir some medical care? And some food? I would say clean clothes, but they might not have his size."

"And a pipe," Fir suggested. "They took my pipe."

"You can't smoke in here."

"We could take him to the doctor, but I think that just a first aid kit and ice pack are probably all that's needed," Jessup said. "I don't know how gnomes feel about medical examination."

"What is medical examination?" Fir repeated to Reg.

"It's... looking at your body to see where you are hurt or sick so that you can be treated. So they can bandage you or give you what you need to mend properly."

He raised white eyebrows high. "We do not need human remedies. Gnomen know proper physic."

Jessup looked from Fir's face to Reg. "He doesn't want a doctor, does he?"

Reg shook her head in agreement. "Why don't you get a first aid kit, then? He'll get whatever kind of traditional healing he needs when we get him out of here."

Jessup was out of the room for just a few minutes, then returned with a small white plastic box of supplies and an ice pack from the freezer. "First, let's get these cuts cleaned up," she suggested, moving closer to Fir and leaning in to examine the injuries. She ripped open a pre-moistened pad and removed it from the foil wrap. "This might sting a bit, but if you just hold still—"

Fir jumped back when she moved it toward him. He grabbed it from her hand and brought it to his nose, sniffing. He made a face and threw it down on the table. "That is not a proper remedy," he accused.

"It's just to help to clean it up and keep it from getting infected," Reg explained. "Sometimes traditional remedies smell bad too, don't they?"

"I know what herbs smell like. That is not safe."

Reg shrugged at Jessup. "Okay. Maybe this wasn't such a good idea. I don't want to accidentally give him something that might do him harm." She turned back to Fir. "How about the ice pack? Just put it against your eye; it will help it to feel better."

He gingerly picked up the ice pack, examined it, squished it around in his hands, then carefully brought it up to his face. He relaxed, holding it there. "This is good," he approved.

"Good. And how about something to eat? Did you get breakfast? It's almost lunchtime now." She looked at her phone. The hours were speeding by. She hoped that Forst and Fir appreciated her efforts.

CHAPTER SIX

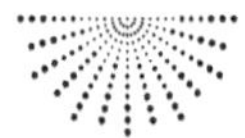

*J*essup did some checking around and managed to get a light lunch in for Fir. He picked up the sandwich and took a big bite out of it, then gagged and spat it back out on his plate. Reg gasped, shocked, and started forward.

"What is it? Are you okay?"

He opened the sandwich and looked inside. With an expression of revulsion, he pulled out the layers of processed meat, leaving just a tomato slice and some limp lettuce. "Gnomen do not eat creatures!"

"Oh, I'm sorry. I didn't know." Reg looked at Jessup. "Did you know?"

In spite of her complexion, Jessup had turned slightly pink. "I… might have heard gnomes were vegetarian," Jessup said, looking at the meat Fir had disposed of, "but I don't deal with gnomes very often. I didn't think of it. I'm sorry," she addressed Fir, "I didn't mean to give you something you don't eat."

He gave a curt nod and bit into the sandwich.

Reg looked over at Jessup. "So, any progress being made on getting him out of here?"

"I think it will work out. Someone should be here to tell us… hopefully, it won't be too much longer."

"And what about my plot?" Fir asked. "I am going back to my living."

"Uh… I don't know." Reg raised an eyebrow at Jessup. "He is going to go back to where he's been living. What's going to happen if he does that?"

"He'll probably be arrested again for trespassing. Or vagrancy. Whatever it takes to get him back off of it again so that they proceed with the development." She shrugged. "There's not much we can do about that. They have all of the appropriate permits, so it is going ahead, whether Mr. Blumenthal likes it or not."

Reg frowned. She shook her head. "There must be a way to stop it."

"Sometimes there are ways… but I don't think you're going to find any way to get them to stop at this point. All of that has to be addressed during the public hearings that happened long before this. Any objectors are expected to speak up and voice their opinions then."

"But Fir can't talk in a forum like that."

"That's the law. He could have taken an interpreter or someone to speak for him. But if he doesn't have any objection during those stages, he's missed the boat. It isn't like it is a historical site, or native land, or a graveyard. They are going to go ahead with development."

"What if… how about if there was a rare species discovered there? Some animal habitat… Then they would have to stop, wouldn't they?"

She'd heard of such things on TV. Maybe they could put some rare species there, or at least tell the authorities that they had seen one, which would give them the time to cook up something more permanent. The developers would have to take a few days at least to either confirm or refute the claim.

"Hmm." Jessup shrugged with one shoulder. "It's a possibility, I guess. But you can't go to the police with that. You'll have to find the proper authority. Department of the Environment maybe. And you'll have to do it quickly because they have probably started by now. I can't see them waiting around once Mr. Blumenthal was out of the way. They'd know that he might not be in jail for very long. If he really were an activist, he probably would have been out early this morning."

Reg's stomach knotted. She had hoped to get a jump on the developers, but Jessup was probably right. They had probably started bulldozing the moment Fir had been arrested. She pulled out her phone and looked at it. Finding the proper government agency could be complicated. She was sure to end up mired in the bureaucracy. Even government organizations that tried to be transparent and accessible usually ended up being so complicated that it was impossible for Joe Blow off the street to sort it out.

"Tell me about the plants and animals in your garden. Do you have anything rare? That there isn't much left of in the world?"

Fir considered the question. He put down his half-eaten sandwich and licked his fingers.

"Humans like to kill plants."

"Yes... but not the last of a species. They try not to wipe something off of the earth forever."

"There is the white glory. Humans call it beach clustervine. Very hard to find now. Not many places left that it can grow."

"Perfect. Beach clustervine." Reg considered her plan of attack. She looked over at Jessup. "You might want to go for a walk."

"What?"

"I think... you might not want to hear what I'm going to say. You should go for a walk, stretch your legs, see how things are coming along out there. Tell them that Mr. Blumenthal is ready to go home and is talking about calling... a lawyer or some advocacy group."

Jessup got slowly to her feet. "Just what do you have in mind?"

"Didn't I just tell you that you don't want to know? Why would you ask?"

The policewoman still hesitated. But after looking at Reg for another minute, she finally decided to go with what Reg had said and made herself scarce. She left the room. Fir watched Reg curiously, his eyes bright. He was eager to get home, but he was interested in what she was doing.

Reg did a quick internet search and called the local TV station. She bullied her way through the gatekeepers and, in a few minutes, was talking with Buzz Rockwell—his real name—who was the go-to news anchor for Black Sands news.

"It's a human-interest story," Reg said. "Big corporation versus the environment. But you need to get on it right away and get a camera crew going, or it's going to be too late to stop the destruction."

"What exactly do you have?" Buzz asked cautiously.

"A developer has had the police arrest the last of the squatters on their property and is ready to destroy one of the last places on earth where beach clustervine grows wild."

"What is that?"

"It's a plant. An endangered species. This is one of the only places in the world clustervine grows. If they raze it for a new highway and housing development, they are doing incalculable damage to the environment. Besides the fact that they are taking homes away from the indigent and using their size to commit injustices."

"Where is this? Can you meet me there? Show me the plant in question? We'll need proof before we start throwing accusations around."

"I'll get over there when I can, but right now, I'm trying to get this man out of jail. He's the only one who can show you where it is growing."

Reg described the best she could where Fir's patch was and emphasized again how they had nearly run him over with the bulldozer and would have the plant swept out of existence before anyone could stop them if Buzz delayed getting there.

After some more discussion, Buzz agreed to get his camera crew over there to see if he could stop the development. Reg would continue to work on freeing Fir and would join Buzz as soon as she could so that they could show him and the developers the location of the rare flowering vine.

Reg hung up, then looked over at Fir, wondering what he would think of her approach.

He gave her a bright smile. "You are very good at outside talking."

Reg laughed. "Yes, I've got a mouth on me. I'll admit that!"

"You will get me back to my patch?"

"Sooner or later. Hopefully, sooner."

On cue, the door was opened by a policeman Reg hadn't yet met. He was wearing a uniform that was slightly different from the others Reg had seen. No duty belt; he was not on the front lines fighting crime in Black Sands. He was an older, balding man, on the short side, but not nearly as short as Fir and Forst. He smiled reassuringly and sat in one of the empty seats.

"Hi, my name is Darcy. I'm sorry for all of the trouble that you've been through. I'm here to see that everything is straightened out."

Reg raised her brows. "I'll believe that when I see it."

"I want to thank you for advocating for Mr. Blumenthal. It is important that someone stand up for the... less fortunate in our society. For those who are not as able to speak for themselves."

Reg thought that was an insensitive thing to say in front of Fir, but she said nothing, sitting back with her eyebrows raised waiting for Darcy to explain what he was going to do for them. She didn't need any false praise. She didn't need cops pretending that they cared about what happened to Fir Blumenthal. If they had the kind of environment where all people were treated with respect and the presumption of innocence, they wouldn't be where they were, and Fir would not have a black eye.

"I'm sorry it has taken so long for us to mobilize and get into a position where we can help you. It doesn't usually take that long. Thank you for your patience."

Fir looked at Reg. "What does this human want?"

"He wants to make sure you don't sue him," Reg returned, speaking aloud so that Darcy could hear her. "He's just trying to cover his butt now."

"I can understand your perspective," Darcy admitted. "I hope that you will accept our apologies and understand that we have the greatest respect for the citizens of Black Sands and have no desire to see injustices done. Mr. Blumenthal was in an awkward position, and perhaps it could have been handled better. I'm just glad that we could figure this out right away and get on top of it now."

"So how are you on top of it? Are you ready to let him go?"

Darcy hesitated for a moment, maybe deciding just how much more smoke he should try to blow in Reg's direction. He rightly concluded that his approach wasn't getting anywhere with Reg. She'd been involved with too many police officers and in too many other sticky situations to believe anything that came out of his mouth.

"We believe that there has been a misunderstanding with Mr. Blumenthal," Darcy said slowly. "The officers at the scene were led to believe that he was a saboteur when perhaps he was only exercising his right to free speech... at any rate, we greatly regret that he suffered an injury while in the cell and that more action wasn't taken to facilitate communication... Maybe if he had asked for you when he was first arrested... if he had a card saying that he needed assistance or to call you in the event of an emergency..."

"So you're letting him go?" Reg demanded.

"Uh... yes. We will see to his immediate release. Again, if we had realized at the time..." Darcy trailed off, unable to give a full explanation. He shrugged dramatically. "I'm sorry for any distress..."

"Just get his possessions and get us signed out. He would like to be able to get back to his home before it is bulldozed into the ground."

Darcy tugged at his uniform collar. "Yes, of course. I hope that no permanent harm has been done…"

"Oh, you'll hear from us about that."

Darcy looked at her for another moment, his face pale and grave. Then he got up and retreated. Off to get Fir's possessions and get them on their way, she hoped.

Fir looked relieved. He nodded his head vigorously at Reg. "Yes, you are very good with outside words," he complimented her again. "You know how to talk to humans."

"Some humans. I'll drive you back to your plot, and talk to the TV guy and developers, and hopefully, that will mean a temporary stay to the development while they figure out what they have to do. They should be required to protect the habitat of the clustervine, but I don't know how much space they will have to leave around it, whether it's just the plant itself, or a wider area…"

"More than one plant," Fir advised. "A colony."

"Oh, good. That should give you more space, then. They'll have to protect the colony somehow."

"Humans protecting plants?" he asked skeptically and shook his head. As far as he was concerned, humans were in the business of harming plants, not saving them. A position that was usually true. Reg had to admit that while she enjoyed walking through a garden or hiking through a wilderness area, she never gave much thought to the plants themselves and who tended them or what their needs were.

Did plants have feelings? Did they know Fir cared for them? It had never occurred to her that they might have any level of sentience, but Fir's attitude toward them was more like a parent for a child than someone who just watered and fertilized plants.

"Of course plants have feeling," Fir said, a wrinkle in his brow.

Reg hadn't realized that she'd been so open with her thoughts. "I never knew that. What kind of feelings do they have?"

Fir's eyes rolled toward the ceiling as he considered. "They have likes and not. They know who cares for them. They can be hurt." He looked back at her again, checking to make sure she understood.

"That's amazing. I never knew that. I thought they were just… inanimate."

Fir shook his head like she was being foolish. "They are living things," he pointed out. "They are not dead."

*J*essup was the one who returned with Fir's possessions and had him make sure everything was there. She looked sideways at Reg. "So… did you get everything you needed?"

"Sure. We'll head over and have a little chat with the developers next. Then we'll see who's going to be bulldozing people's plants."

"Good luck. I hope everything works out. I don't like it when there are conflicts between the police department and the other races. I wish we had a better interface, but when most of the police officers are non-practitioners, it's impossible to make sure that they don't step on any toes. You can't exactly tutor them in the rights of other species."

"They can still do better than this. It's ridiculous that they would jail someone like Fir without making sure that his needs were met and he wasn't victimized. It's obvious he is vulnerable to people who are bigger and stronger than him and that he doesn't have the ability to ask for help."

Jessup shrugged uncomfortably. "Your perspective is different when you're a cop facing a potentially dangerous criminal. You see things differently."

Reg looked at Fir and couldn't believe that anyone would think he was dangerous. Yes, he had done some damage to industrial equipment, but he hadn't been causing anyone physical harm. He wasn't big enough to hurt anyone.

Fir made a mark where Jessup indicated on the release form, and Reg leaned closer to study it. "Is that… your name?"

Fir nodded. "It is the rune for my family. What we use for identifying our territory and property."

"Cool. I've never seen a mark like that before. Except maybe on some fantasy show on TV."

"TV?"

Reg cleared her throat. "Never mind. Let's go. I'll drive you home if you show me the way."

* * *

It had been a long day. Reg had not been planning to take so much time aiding a gnome in distress. But she felt good that she had. Fir had been so delighted to return to his garden plot and had immediately taken her to see the clustervine and several other favorite plants. She'd had a hard time disengaging from him, explaining that she had to go home to her own duties. He doffed his cap to her, bowing several times in thanks for all she had done. Buzz the TV anchor was in full swing with his camera crew, getting plenty of close-ups of the white flowers and the machinery operators as they mopped red faces and considered the little plants that threatened to derail their plans. Buzz thanked Reg for the tip. She advised him that Fir would not be doing an interview, but she was sure he would show Buzz around his little plot and show him all of the places that needed to be protected from the bulldozers of the eager developer.

"He doesn't speak," she warned for the third time, "so don't pressure him. It isn't because he's camera shy or obstinate; he just isn't very verbal."

"I understand. We can work with that. He won't be the first

interviewee I've had who won't speak with the cameras on him."

"He won't speak with them off, either. Maybe a word or two, but don't expect a conversation, even off the record."

"I can handle it, Ms. Rawlins, I promise."

"Okay. Because he's going to tell me if you harass him. And I'm going to watch the coverage."

"We'll be very respectful. There's nothing to worry about. This is a great David versus Goliath story. We'll make the most of it."

"Good."

On her return home, Reg went around to Sarah's garden to see if Forst was still there. She didn't see him at first, but when she turned to go, saw a red cap out of the corner of her eye and turned back for a second look. She found him sitting on a tree stump, blending in so well with his surroundings that she thought at first she was seeing things.

"Is it well?" he asked immediately. "Did you get him out of the cage?"

"He is out of the cage and back home on his plot. We're fighting back against the humans who want to destroy his garden. Hopefully, that will work out, and he'll be able to keep some of it unspoiled."

"Oh, thank you!" He jumped up from his rock and ran to her, giving her a vigorous hug. "You are a gnomen champion! Much joy to the gnomen!"

"Well... thank you!" Reg tried to return the hug, bending down and patting him on the shoulder and back. "I'm glad I could help."

"This is wonderful news. Wonderful."

Reg nodded. "It is. And I... need to go back in now, and do my own work."

"Yes, yes. Tend to your living," he agreed. He made shooing motions for her to go back into the cottage. "Your cat has been watching us very carefully."

"He's probably wondering what you're up to. He's very curious."

Forst turned and surveyed the ruined garden, hands on hips. "There is much to do here. I must tend these plants."

Reg waved and headed back to the cottage. "See you later, then."

* * *

Back in the house, she made herself a cheese sandwich, thinking as she laid a slice of tomato on the cheese about the plant that had borne the fruit. Were plants happy to have their fruit picked? Did it hurt? Did they understand the animal's need for nourishment? Did they feel frustrated when humans kept taking their fruit? Or was she assigning them too much sentience? Fir hadn't sounded like they had a complex thought process, just feelings about the things around them. But Reg wondered how far that went.

She sent a little prayer of thanks in the direction of whatever tomato vine had supplied that part of her lunch, and sat down to eat it. Starlight rubbed against her legs, purring and seeking affection. She petted him with her toes, not wanting to get cat fur in her food. The phone rang. Reg put down her sandwich and dug her phone out of her pocket to answer it.

"Hello?"

"Regina! It is Francesca."

"Oh, hi. I saw you called earlier, but I was at the police station and had a lot to deal with."

"Oh—is everything all right?"

"Yes. Just helping someone out. What's going on?" The worried tone in Francesca's voice alerted her that all was not well. She hoped that her failure to answer Francesca's earlier call hadn't resulted in something terrible happening.

"It is the kattakyns. They are gone!"

"Gone?" Reg sat up straight, immediately alert. "What do you mean, they are gone? All of them? Where did they go? It isn't... someone who wants to get the Witch Doctor back, is it?"

"I do not think so. But I cannot feel him, so I do not know

what is going on. All I know is, when I went to find the cats today, they were gone. Nicole is here, but the kittens have disappeared."

"Inside the house? Outside? You didn't let them all outside, did you?" Reg had been critical of Francesca letting Nicole run freely outside. She couldn't fathom that anyone would let nine kittens, especially ones bound to a dangerous Witch Doctor, to run free.

"No, they were in the house. I did not put them out. But I cannot find them. I have looked in all of the places that they normally play and sleep, but they are not there."

"Oh, dear. I hope nothing has happened to them. What if the binding spell didn't hold, and they all… got together and re-formed the Witch Doctor?"

"Can you not feel him?" Francesca asked.

"Oh… well, I could before." Reg took a moment to see if she could feel the Witch Doctor. She didn't feel the anxiety and dread that she had previously felt whenever he had been around. "I don't feel him. But what if he is blocking me because he knows that I can feel him? What if he's already back again and is being more careful this time?"

"I do not think that is the case. I am very sure of my spell. He could not have broken it again already. It will hold for hundreds of years."

"What if someone else severed it or broke it? What if he has an accomplice that we didn't know about?"

"You could come over here? Then you can see what you think. If you can feel him and if you think there was someone else here."

"I don't know if I can do all of that…" Reg sighed. She was exhausted after the trip to the police station and now she was expected to go out again and play Ghostbusters. "I guess I'll come over… but I don't know if I'll be able to feel anything. I'm pretty tired."

"I will wait for you. I will give you the address."

"Okay, yeah." Reg turned her phone to speaker mode and navigated to the maps app to input it.

CHAPTER EIGHT

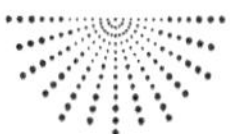

"I do not know what could have happened to them," Francesca said when she opened the door. She had worry lines across her forehead, unusual for the pretty blond who usually looked so carefree and had preached to Reg that cats needed to roam outside for their health.

"Well, let's look around, and I'll see if I can sense anything."

She walked into the house. Francesca had previously confided that she didn't like the feeling in her home, that it was too dark and she hadn't been able to make it feel any better. Reg thought again that Francesca should get Corvin to cast some of his magic there. He did house blessings. Now that she knew Francesca was a practitioner, she could talk about it openly, where before she could only hint at it.

Francesca was right. It did feel dark and cold, in spite of her efforts to decorate it to look light and airy, and having boosted the lighting. Reg closed her eyes and opened up her senses, seeing what she could feel.

Nicole walked into the room. Reg immediately felt waves of confusion. She opened her eyes and looked at Nicole. "Don't you know what happened to them either, Nicole?" She bent over to pet Nicole. After sniffing her hand, Nicole deigned to be petted.

She rubbed Reg's legs and went to Francesca and back to Reg again.

"She must know something about it," Reg suggested. "She's been very interested in their care. She must have been keeping an eye on them, don't you think?"

Francesca nodded. She picked Nicole up.

"What about it, Nicole? Where are they?"

Nicole rubbed the top of her head against Francesca's chin. Reg focused on the cat, feeling discomfited.

"What is it?" Francesca asked, noticing Reg's expression. "Do you think you know something? Has someone been here? You cannot feel the Witch Doctor?"

"No, I still can't feel him. The thing is… I'm not getting any sadness from Nicole."

"Oh?"

"If the kittens are lost or ran away, then she should be sad, shouldn't she? She was acting like a mother cat toward them. She was bonding with them. So when they disappear, she should be sad."

"Yes. I would expect so. But you said that you are tired. Maybe this is just your tiredness."

Reg shook her head. "No. Something isn't right here."

She started looking around the room, checking the closet and under the furniture, trying to seek for lost objects as she had done so many times in the past. She had not been able to successfully seek since Sarah's emerald had disappeared, but she hoped that it would work anyway. The kittens were a significant presence. They should not be hard to find.

Francesca was quiet as Reg went into the kitchen, and into each of the bedrooms on the main floor. Reg looked everywhere she could think of that the kittens could be hiding.

"Is there an attic? A basement?"

"No basement," Francesca said, shaking her head. There were few basements built in Black Sands because of the high water table. "But there is an attic."

She went down the hallway and reached up for a cord in the ceiling where there was an access panel. Nicole, following her owner, nipped at her ankles, drawing a shriek of surprise and pain from Francesca.

"Ow! What are you doing, Nicole? Ouch, you do not bite me!"

She bent over, rubbing her ankles and scowling at the cat. Reg looked thoughtfully up at the attic access. Nicole, slinking away out of Francesca's reach, started to move toward Reg.

"No, you don't," she warned. "Don't bite me."

She grabbed the cord and pulled, causing a set of stairs to fold down into the hallway. Nicole folded back her ears and hissed. Francesca was shaking her head at Nicole's behavior. "What has gotten into you?"

Reg climbed the stairs. There was a light switch at the top of the stairs, and she flicked it on.

The attic was nearly empty. A few dusty boxes and some construction materials, but most of it was wide-open to Reg's gaze. And out from behind the boxes, she saw several sets of eyes in little black faces looking back at her.

"They're up here."

Francesca came up the stairs and looked. "There they are! The naughty kitties! How did they get up here? I didn't have the stairs pulled down at all."

Reg looked around for some clue. "Maybe they came up the ventilation ducts? Are there any vents that are not covered with a grill?"

"I do not think so… I guess we must look." Francesca climbed the stairs the rest of the way and went toward the kittens. "Back down you go!" she told them, shooing them with her hands toward the stairs. "Get out. Not allowed to be in the attic. Out you go!"

Reg went back down the stairs and saw Nicole waiting at the bottom, counting the kittens as they went by her. Nicole glared at Reg, waves of anger coming off of her. Reg stood there looking at her, trying to understand what was going on. Francesca finished shooing the kittens down from the attic and returned down the stairs after Reg.

"I think Nicole knows you're going to send the kittens to other homes."

Francesca shook her head. "How would she know that?"

"She's been around when we've discussed it. I didn't think she understood… but I guess she does."

"She is just acting like a mother cat. Moving her kittens around to keep them safe. It is instinct."

"I don't think so. I think she knows exactly what she's doing."

* * *

For a few days, things seemed almost normal. Corvin stayed away. There were no more appearances of the Witch Doctor or any other evil influences. Reg had a few readings with clients, but nothing that taxed her too much or had weird results. She could almost convince herself that the strange events that had taken place in the time that she'd been in Black Sands had just been a dream or something she had imagined.

Reg saw Forst occasionally in the garden. Sometimes he was there, puttering around, tying up plants, talking to them, digging around them. At other times, he seemed to be absent, neglecting his duties, or maybe off to the store to pick up something he needed, or visiting Fir, who was enjoying the peace and quiet of his plot, undisturbed by the bulldozers that stood idle outside the perimeter that Florida Fish and Wildlife had set up to protect the rare ecosystem. It wasn't any of her business what Forst did. As long as Sarah was happy with the results, it didn't matter how much time he spent in the garden and how much he was absent from it.

She hadn't heard him crying again. But he did occasionally mutter to himself, looking out over the garden with his hands on his hips, trying to work through some knotty problem.

Starlight was sitting in the windowsill in the bedroom and started to meow, calling out to Reg in the voice that meant he wanted her attention for something. Reg set down her teacup and headed back to the bedroom to see what was going on. Was Nicole back in the garden again? Reg wouldn't be surprised if Francesca had let her out, considering her views on proper cat care. If Sarah caught Nicole in the garden again, Reg wasn't sure what she would do. She likewise didn't know how Forst would react to a cat in his territory. He wouldn't eat her, but not all of the magical beings Reg had met so far liked cats. In fact, few of them did.

She got to the window and scratched Starlight's ears. "What is it, Star? Is Nicole back?" She peered out the window, and her attention was caught, not by a black cat, but by Forst dancing around wildly. He whooped as he jumped up and down. "What's going on? Is it a spell?"

Starlight pressed his nose to the window, watching with great interest.

"Well… I guess I'll go find out what's going on. You don't think I'll be interrupting, do you? Will he be angry or embarrassed if I go out there?"

Starlight didn't give any sign that he understood or had an answer for her.

Reg went out to the garden, looking around the corner tentatively, worried that she might be interrupting something private. "Uh… Forst…?"

He looked at her and stopped dancing, but was still smiling broadly.

"What's going on?"

"I found it! I have been looking for days, and I finally found it!"

"What did you find?"

He brandished an object. "A key."

It was dark with corrosion. Too large for a modern house or car key. An old-fashioned key with an ornate handle. Reg raised her eyebrows, looking at it. "Well… I guess you did. Is that a good thing? Had you lost it?"

"Something was disturbing this garden. I could feel something… blocking the growth, casting a darkness over the plants, keeping it in the shadows. But I could not tell what it was or to find the offending object."

"And this is it? This was causing the problem?"

Forst nodded, his cheeks bright pink, looking immensely satisfied with himself.

"Can I see it?" Reg asked, drawn to the innocuous key, somehow the cause of Forst's difficulties rehabilitating the garden.

Forst looked at it for a moment, then handed it to Reg. "You can change cursed objects?" he asked.

"Is it really cursed?" Reg held the key in the palm of her hand, weighing it and studying it carefully. If didn't look cursed. She didn't feel a sense of evil from it as Forst did. It didn't burn her hand or buzz with energy. It just looked like an old key, buried there years before, allowed to rust in the damp ground.

Quite the contrary, she felt drawn toward it. She felt like it was hers, and that she needed to find the lock it belonged to. It was her fate to unlock that lock and take the treasure that it secured.

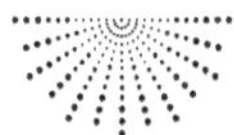

As much as Reg felt drawn to the key, it wasn't hers, and it wasn't up to her to decide what to do with it. She couldn't see Sarah wanting it, but she needed to at least check. She told Forst that she would take it to Sarah in the big house, and he nodded, unconcerned with what she did with it, as long as it wasn't disturbing the forces in the garden. He was happy to get rid of it.

Reg knocked on the back door and walked into the kitchen. "Sarah, are you home?"

"Upstairs," Sarah called back. Reg mounted the stairs and followed the sounds of movement to discover Sarah in her bedroom, tearing through drawers full of clothes, scattering them here and there as she looked for something.

"Spring cleaning?" Reg suggested.

"You wouldn't believe how many clothes I have in this house! I am looking for something…" she tossed a few more items around, "something a little younger. I don't feel like old fogey clothes, not since I woke up. I want brighter colors, trendier styles. What is popular again? I have years and years' worth of clothes; there must be something that will look sharp."

"I don't know," Reg admitted. She gravitated toward clothes

that fit her medium/fortune-teller persona: the long flowing skirts, a headscarf around her box braids, breezy fabrics. They weren't fashionable or trendy. That wasn't the persona she was trying to project. "You could check some internet sites. Or go to a place where younger people hang around."

"I suppose so," Sarah agreed. She continued to plow through the drawers.

"Forst found something in the garden, and we were wondering about it."

"Oh? What did he find in the garden?"

Reg held up the key. "This. An old key."

Sarah peered at her. "Curious. I don't recognize it. I don't think it was ever mine. I've been here for a long time, so I'm not sure who else could have lost it here."

"Do you want it?"

"Want it? Why would I want it, dear?"

"It's your property. It was found in your garden. I would kind of like to have it, but I didn't want to claim it, in case it was something you wanted."

"If you like it, you can have it. I don't know why you would."

"Forst says that it was causing problems with your garden. The plants will grow better now that it has been taken out."

Sarah stopped and looked at it, picked it up from Reg's hand, examined it, and put it back down again. "Gnomes have different magic... I can't see or feel anything."

"I don't either. I actually really like it. It looks cool."

"It's filthy. Maybe it will look nice when you clean it and remove all of the corrosion, shine it up. But right now... I'm not sure what you see in it."

"Neither am I! But it's intriguing. I wonder what kind of lock it was meant to open."

* * *

Back in the cottage, Reg washed the dirt off of the key, then looked for metal polish in the cupboards. She couldn't find anything, so she tried an internet search instead, seeing what she could use to concoct her own metal polish. Maybe some steel wool to help to rub the corrosion off of the key.

The phone rang. Irritated, Reg answered the call. "Hello?"

"Miss Rawlins. This is Davyn Smithy. I don't know if you remember me…"

"Of course I do. You're the one who conducted Corvin's hearing."

"Yes, that's right."

"I don't think I need anything from you. I was not impressed with the way you handled that hearing. You weren't exactly on my side."

"I wasn't supposed to be on your side," Davyn pointed out. "I was supposed to be impartial."

"And I don't think you were. I think you were squarely on Corvin's side and did the best you could to get him off, even if it meant smearing my name."

"I'm sorry you saw it that way. That isn't the way it was intended."

"Huh. I think I was lucky that Corvin was disciplined at all, after the way you ran the hearing. At least the tribunal wasn't fooled."

"I was part of that tribunal. We did what we felt was right."

"What do you want, Dave?" Reg demanded bluntly.

He was silent for a moment, perhaps shocked by her attitude. "The fact is, we have been asked to review Corvin Hunter's case in light of recent events. Since his sentence was indefinite, we as a committee are required to review it on occasion to see if the requirements of the disciplinary action have been met…"

"You want to end his discipline. The shunning by the coven."

"We don't want to end his discipline. We are in a position where we need to consider what the appropriate action would be. Has he met the terms of the sentence, or do we need to continue?"

"You need to continue. Do you really think he's reformed? That he's somehow turned himself around in just this short time and is ready to be a contributing member of society again?"

"That is the question. It has been suggested that his defeat of the Witch Doctor was a service to the community and that this altruistic gesture demonstrated not just how much the community needs him, but also how he is willing to serve its needs…"

"It has been suggested? Do you mean that Corvin has suggested it? I can't see anyone else being fooled into thinking that he was doing something for anyone else. There was nothing altruistic about his actions."

"Since you were there, and since you have… experience with him and were the person who was most affected by his breaches of our code…"

"What?"

"I was hoping that you would be open to meeting together so that I could get your thoughts and feelings on his progress."

"You want my thoughts and feelings about his progress? He hasn't made any. He's just manipulating you."

"Could we meet?"

"My feelings aren't going to change."

"No, but I could get some more details. What happened with the Witch Doctor and the draugrs? I have one side of the story, but that is just one side, and there are going to be several views of what happened and what Corvin's motives were. I want to be able to go through some of your thoughts."

Ugh. Reg was not ready to meet with Davyn Smithy. As far as she was concerned, he was just a fanboy of Corvin's. He wasn't going to take her opinion seriously. He was going through the motions and would discharge Corvin's penalty once he finished his interviews.

"I'm not interested…"

"So you don't want any input into whether his punishment continues or not?"

"I've given my comments."

"Okay…" Davyn trailed off.

Reg's stomach rebelled, swishing around so that she thought she would be sick. "Oh, fine. But it had better be quick, and I'd better not hear anything out of your mouth that suggests that what he did was my fault."

"No, of course not."

As if that weren't what he had already suggested at Corvin's hearing. Now that they were in private, where there weren't other people to hear and be influenced by what he said, things would be different.

* * *

Reg looked over the profiles that Francesca had prepared on the people who were interested in adopting the draugr kittens. It was all very professionally done like they were job candidates. Headshots, biographies, background checks, everything pulled together into a concise portfolio for each individual. Reg looked away from the papers and watched the kittens playing and interacting with Nicole.

"Why don't you give me your impressions of each one," she suggested, "and I'll think about the kittens and which ones might fit with each person."

"I have written down everything you need to know," Francesca pointed out impatiently.

Reg wasn't about to say that she couldn't read that much information in the time they had arranged for, or that she didn't have the patience to work through that much text no matter how much time she had. She had learned that there was always a way to get around reading if she were creative enough.

"This is about intuition, not portfolios," she told Francesca. "You can have the best resume in the world and still be wrong for the job. You've been talking and emailing with these guys, so you have come to some conclusions already, even if you think you've kept an open mind. It's my job to dig into those impressions and match up the kattakyns' personalities, right?"

Francesca nodded reluctantly. She'd obviously put a lot of work into the profiles and didn't like to abandon them so easily. So Reg made a show of leafing through them, frowning as she studied the names and faces, and putting them into a new order. None of it mattered, it was a show to make Francesca feel like her work was appreciated and an essential part of the process. Reg sighed, squared all of the papers in one pile, and pointed to the one at the top of the pile.

"I'm interested in this guy. How did he come across to you?"

Francesca was eager to talk once Reg had validated the process. "Yes, I thought he was an excellent candidate too. He is in Egypt, and you know the history of Egypt and cats."

Reg didn't know much. She knew that they had worshiped cats and drawn them in hieroglyphs, so that must mean that they respected them. Or at least that they didn't eat them. She nodded thoughtfully.

"He is a respected warlock, leader of his coven. I have heard about him before, through several sources. Always good things."

"And he doesn't already have a familiar?"

"He did until recently. A very old cat, Massud, who passed away just recently."

"So, this wouldn't be his first cat."

"No. Exactly. He already knows how to care for a cat and has all of the equipment and food. No suggestion that he was ever abusive or negligent. Highly respected. And since Massud lived to an old age, he obviously is a good caregiver."

Reg watched the black kittens. "If he's had an old cat, how do you think he's going to manage a kitten? They're a lot more active and get into things."

Francesca considered this, biting her lip. "That's true," she agreed. "So maybe he's not such a good match…"

"He has to expect that any replacement for Massud is going to be a lot more energetic. But maybe we should match him with one of the quieter kittens. Not little Nico."

Francesca glanced over at them. "Which one is he?"

Reg was still amazed that Francesca couldn't tell the kittens apart. It was true that they were all black without any markings, but they were different sizes and body types, with widely varying personalities. Francesca was with them more than Reg was, she should have been able to see some of the differences.

"Over there…"

Francesca's head swiveled as she followed Reg's finger to the black kitten currently halfway up the drapes.

"Oh. Yes, I think you're right. Not Nico. Do you have one in mind, then?"

"I was thinking maybe Horace." Reg indicated the fatter kitten snoozing in the sun on one of the kitchen chairs, positioned in the sunbeam coming through the window.

"Horace." Francesca nodded. She typed something into her computer. "And what should I tell him about Horace?"

"He's quiet. Very intelligent. Likes to think things through. Good at solving problems." Reg waited while Francesca finished typing these thoughts out. "I think he'd be a good match for someone used to an older cat. I don't think he'll tear the house apart like a certain other kattakyn."

Nico, inching his way up the drapes, turned to look at Reg. He hesitated, trying to decide whether she was going to pursue him and pull him down from the curtain. When she didn't move or tell him to come down, he looked back up at this intended destination and kept going.

Reg took the profile for the Egyptian warlock and slid it to the bottom of her pile. "Okay, how about her?" Reg studied the Asian woman's face. "She looks very young." Of course, Reg had discovered a witch's looks didn't always reflect her age. Sarah, who appeared to be in her sixties, was supposed to be hundreds of years old, and Corvin, who Reg wouldn't have guessed to be that much older than she was, was decades older. She didn't know whether magic naturally kept him younger, or if he had some other long-lived race's blood in his veins, or whether he invoked some anti-aging spell. Sarah had a powerful emerald that kept her young and hearty. Reg would not have known that if not for the theft of the emerald. Once the emerald was no longer in Sarah's possession, the aging process had kicked in, and she had gotten very old and frail very quickly.

"She is young," Francesca agreed. "A fairly new practitioner, she comes from families that were not aware of their powers. She seems to have inherited the gene from both parents and is subsequently much stronger than they are. She has good reports from the mentors she has been working with so far. She has a natural affinity for cats, and they think that she would be able to stabilize and control her magic much more quickly with the aid of a cat."

"A stabilizing influence," Reg repeated.

"Yes."

So again, not Nico. Reg sensed that he was going to be hard to place. Just as Reg had been a challenge for Mrs. Bloom to find a long-term placement for, she was going to have to really search to find the right practitioner for Nico.

She closed her eyes and reached out mentally to the kittens. They needed one who would be responsive to a new practitioner's powers and requests. Not one who had his own ideas about what he should do or who would be distracted by a butterfly fluttering by.

She opened her eyes and studied them. A female had stopped playing and was looking at her, interested and responsive. Reg clicked her tongue. "Come here. Come on, Sally."

Sally moved immediately toward Reg, ears pricked up attentively. She padded up to Reg's side and stared up at her, waiting.

"Can you help me?" Reg asked. "I need a boost reaching a friend."

As Reg reached out mentally toward Sarah, for lack of a better plan, Sally stood up on her hind legs and put her front paws on Reg's leg. Reg could immediately feel the sharpening of her senses and an extension to her ability to reach out, like a pair of rabbit ears that helped to clear the picture on an ancient television set. She didn't actually need to get a message to Sarah or to know what she was doing, so after a few moments, she released her energy, and Sally dropped back down onto all fours.

"Sally," Reg told Francesca. "Definitely Sally."

CHAPTER TEN

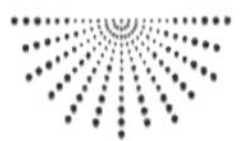

Oddly enough, Davyn Smithy worked out of an insurance office. A bland, dreary sort of a place, thoroughly nonmagical and uninteresting and as far as possible from the dramatic personality he tried to portray within the magical community. He met her wearing a white shirt with blue pinstripes, glasses with thin black rims, and dark slacks. Without his dramatic robes, he looked like an accountant instead of a warlock.

"Good to see you again, Miss Rawlins," he greeted with a polite smile, putting his hand out to shake hers. Reg did not shake. After an awkward moment, he lowered his hand, his neck flushing red around his collar. "I have a meeting room booked for us. Would you like coffee? Water?"

"Coffee. Just black."

He gestured. "This way."

Other people were bustling around the office. No one who took any note of Reg. No one who was expecting anything the least bit magical to happen while she was there. It was reassuring. She was sure there were still things Davyn could do to influence her, but if she kept up her guard, maybe everything would be fine. She would make sure he understood that under no circumstances should they believe what Corvin said about wanting what was best for the community.

They sat down, each with a cup of coffee.

"Let's get this straight right from the start," Reg said flatly. "There is nothing generous or altruistic about Corvin. He does what is best for him, not for anyone else. He'll portray himself in the best light possible, but don't believe it."

"I have known Corvin for a lot longer than you."

"So maybe you're not the best one to see him for what he is. He uses your relationship to pull the wool over your eyes. He laughs at you thinking that you are capable of making an unbiased judgment. Because if you saw him for the predator he is, you would know that he didn't go to that warehouse because he wanted to fight the draugrs and save the community. He went there because he wanted to suck the powers out of the artifacts that the Witch Doctor was smuggling, and eventually, even from the Witch Doctor himself. Do you have any idea how powerful he is now, after drinking all of that in? He's dangerous, and you're just going to turn him loose on the community."

"A decision has not been made. Don't assume that you know what will happen."

"You're telling me you believe what he is saying about saving the city from the Witch Doctor. So it's obvious which way you are going."

"You are jumping to conclusions."

Reg stared at him, meeting his eyes aggressively until he was forced to look away. "I wouldn't have survived this long if I hadn't been able to make snap judgments about what other people are thinking. You want him to be free in the community. You want to talk to him and to discuss business with him. You don't want to have to shun him."

Davyn sighed, looking down into his coffee cup. "All of that is true," he admitted. "But I am not going to make a decision without considering the opinions of everyone involved. I will rule against my own desires and preferences if that is what is best for the magical community."

Reg wondered whether that were true. Even if Corvin agreed to follow the rules of his coven, those rules were still biased against the women he preyed upon. Without any changes in the rules of how he was to conduct himself, women would continue to be victimized, their powers stripped away by him when they didn't understand what he could do. It had happened to Reg. It would happen to others. There was no doubt in her mind.

"So what's going to happen? If you decide that he did what he did because he was trying to protect everyone, then you'll decide that it is of benefit to the community for him to be a full part of it again. And then he'll be able to do what he wants to."

"He will still be expected to follow the rules of the coven and the laws of the land."

"He'll go back to doing what he's been doing all along."

"We don't have the ability to change his nature. The magical community strives to find a balance between allowing the races their own cultural norms and providing for their needs and preventing harm. Obviously, we cannot always protect everyone. We have to balance the rights of one people against the rights of another."

"In nature, there are predators and there are prey. That doesn't mean we let jackals roam the streets and steal children. Our laws make it illegal for people to kill, steal, and rape. *That's* how you protect people. Not by saying 'unless there's a good reason for it.'"

Davyn sat there silently. She didn't know if he was considering what she had said or just waiting for her to finish her tirade.

"I am not justifying anything Corvin has done," Davyn said finally. "But he is different than we are. We can't deny that."

"What are you going to do?"

"I don't know yet. That's why I'm talking with you, talking with other people who have been in contact with him while he has been shunned, visiting with him and talking to him about his plans and how he is going to contribute, and so on. I'll investigate fully, and then I'll make a recommendation to the council of the coven. And they will make a decision about whether to allow him back into full membership in the coven or not."

"You're going to ask him about his plans and expect him to tell you the truth? He'll tell you whatever you want to hear."

"I'm not that naive. I'll be watching for signs of deception. I'll be making my own observations about whether he is being open and honest."

"He won't be. I don't think you know the difference."

"The tribunal did rule against him after the hearing," Davyn pointed out. "I would think you would have some faith in the process after that."

Reg considered. Was it evidence that they were going to do the right thing and not be misled by Corvin's charm? "I'm more inclined to think that was a one-time thing," she admitted. "An anomaly."

"It wasn't. That's the way we work. We're not just spouting ideals and closing our eyes to reality. We understand what Corvin did and that it was wrong. We understand that he has victimized you more than once."

Reg nodded her agreement.

"And yet..." Davyn trailed off.

"What?"

"Even though he has repeatedly shown you his predatory nature, you continue to talk to him and to take on cases with him. You fought the Witch Doctor alongside him, in spite of your history."

"I can't help it if he shows up at my house or calls me on the phone. You know he can use his charms to involve people in things that they wouldn't choose to do otherwise."

"Why did you agree to fight the Witch Doctor?"

"I didn't." Reg's face flushed hot and she looked away from him. "I told him over and over again that I wouldn't. I told him he was on his own. To get someone else to help him."

"And yet, you still ended up in that warehouse with him."

"I had a vision… I saw the draugr that was stalking him and chasing him. I had to get over there to help him. He would have been killed if I hadn't intervened."

"And then you agreed to go after the Witch Doctor."

"It was the only thing left to do." Reg couldn't think of any other way to explain it. She wasn't sure herself how she had finally gotten embroiled in the fight. No matter how hard she fought it, she knew it was inevitable that she would get involved. Harrison had told her so.

Harrison.

Had his involvement been greater than she had thought? Had he pushed her into it, despite his protests that he couldn't do anything to harm another of his kind? He was the one who had told her she would fight the Witch Doctor. He had given her tips on what she needed to do to defeat him. And then he had disappeared. Was he the one who was responsible for Reg joining the fight? If so, what was his motive for wanting her to fight or to defeat the Witch Doctor?

Were they rivals? Enemies? Did they have a past? Old friends? Brothers? And what about the other immortal that Harrison had mentioned? Weston. It turned out that the Witch Doctor had been looking for Weston, even though he wouldn't admit it. And from his words to Reg… maybe Weston had some shared connection with her too. But she didn't like to think that it was true.

"Reg…?"

Reg focused her attention back on Davyn. "What?"

"You said that Corvin's reason for going into the warehouse was to consume the powers of the magical artifacts being stored there."

"Yeah. Exactly."

"How did you know that?"

"He'd said more than once that he needed to get into the warehouse. And when it got down to the fight, his role was to consume as much of the magic as he could so that he would be strong enough to face the Witch Doctor. That was his whole reason for getting into the building. It wasn't to kill the Witch Doctor, that was just a secondary goal. And he took magic from the Witch Doctor directly, too. Put his hands on him and just… sucked it out."

Reg remembered the feeling, being able to sense the flow of magic and sensing the shift when he started to pull directly from the Witch Doctor. It was terrible and frightening, like watching a lion take down a gazelle. Something she could hardly tear her eyes away from, no matter how awful it was.

Reg's fingers itched. She fidgeted. She slid her hand into the pocket of her skirt and touched the old key there. It was comforting in her hand. She pictured herself using it. Just what did it unlock? What kind of power or wealth would be hers if she could find the lock it would open?

"You don't think that Corvin would have fought the Witch Doctor just to protect the people of Black Sands. You think the only reason he faced him was to get the Witch Doctor's hoard and to take away his power."

Reg had been distracted by the touch of the key. She turned her eyes back to Davyn. "That's right. He wouldn't have done anything just to help a few insignificant people. He wanted power. That was the only reason he was there."

Davyn tapped a pen against the table, ticking away the time. His eyes were far away. How long had he known Corvin? Had they been boys together? Both were, Reg had been told, much older than they looked. Maybe not as old as centuries-old Sarah, but significantly older than their thirtyish bodies led her to believe. They might have been friends for decades, devoted to each other.

"Is there anything else?" Davyn asked eventually. "Are there other things I should be aware of? Since you have been in contact with him and the rest of the coven has not, you may know of things that we have no idea of."

"He's still trying to steal my powers. Even after all he

consumed at the warehouse, the massive amount of magic that he is holding now, he is still trying to steal mine."

Davyn rubbed the stubble of his beard. She had previously thought this was an affectation, that he wanted to appear wise before the others of his coven. But maybe it was just an unconscious gesture.

"Why would he still want your powers? He should be sated."

"Yeah, you would think so, wouldn't you? He compared me to dessert."

Davyn's lips twitched into a slight smile. "Dessert?"

"That even though he's full, he still wants... my powers too. For some reason, I guess they are sweeter to him."

"Because he has already held them once?"

"I guess. I don't understand it all. I don't understand my own powers, much less how it feels for him to hold them. And how he can hold so many other powers at the same time. It seems like... there should be a natural balance, a point at which he can't consume any more, or there is some... negative effect to consuming more. You know what I mean? With food, if you eat too much, you throw up."

Davyn shrugged. "I don't think any of us can understand it, only another one like him."

"Like his father?"

"I told you that warlocks like him are rare. We don't have others to ask. Others like him who would tell us what is fair punishment and what is not. How much he can control and how much is instinctual. Whether all warlocks of his nature would behave the same way, or whether that is just Corvin. We have the old texts, and have referred to them as much as possible, but they have always been feared. Others do their best to avoid them, not to document their histories."

"You can't just accept him back again. You can't say that after all that he's done, that a few weeks of shunning is punishment enough."

"But the verdict did not say how much he needed to be

punished. It said that he had to be a contributing member of the community. And when he is performing a service like he did, even if it is the side effect of pursuing his own goals, that is a great benefit to the community, and those who didn't want him to be shunned in the first place are lobbying to have him reinstated."

"Don't they fear what he can do?"

"Of course… but as long as his target is someone else, it is easy for people to forget their fear. And even if he is being shunned, that does not protect anyone from him. The only thing that would protect everyone would be if he was bound. And that would be a lot more difficult."

"The Witch Doctor could be bound."

"Corvin has more power than the Witch Doctor. He is the only one who could overcome the Witch Doctor because he is the only one who can increase his powers that much. Who else is left?"

"Then why don't you banish him? Send him away. Tell him he's not welcome in the community."

"We can tell him that, of course, but we can't force him to leave." Davyn held her gaze until Reg was forced to look away.

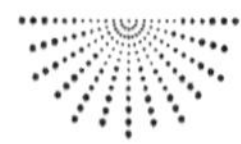

*R*eg did not feel very comforted as she left the insurance office. Davyn's words weighed down on her. Whether they allowed Corvin to be a full participant in the community or not was really an academic question. It provided him with society, but would have no effect on his powers. Even working together, the community might not be powerful enough to bind him or have any control over him.

If he chose to run rampant…

She walked slowly to her car, holding on to the old key. It was warm in her hand and drew her mind away from Corvin and the problem of not being able to control him. She couldn't help dreaming about what it might open. She had always been poor, on the edge of homelessness. Things had been going well for her since she had arrived at Black Sands, but she was still mindful that that could change in a moment. If Jessup decided to arrest her, or the people she served decided she was a scammer, or if they came after her for some crime, real or imagined, then she would once again be on her own, with nothing to her name but a cat with psychic powers, a car that barely ran, and whatever she could throw in a suitcase before she disappeared.

If the key unlocked a treasure, she would be rich. She could be wealthy enough never to have to worry about being out on the street again. She had seen the Witch Doctor's hoard, how he had gathered so much of magical value. There were other hoards like that. Kings and pharaohs had amassed untold wealth. And those treasures had not all been discovered. There were myths of secret treasures and lands that disappeared from the knowledge of men, but they could still be out there somewhere, if she had a way to find and access them. Like a magical key.

She had to let go of the key to start her car and drive home and, as she did, the problem of Corvin once again slid into her mind. Who could defeat him? Could Harrison? They said he was an immortal, like the Witch Doctor. She knew that his powers were far greater than anything Corvin had been able to wield before defeating the Witch Doctor. But now that he had the Witch Doctor's power, were they equals? Or was Harrison still stronger? What would happen if the two faced each other?

* * *

When Reg got into the yard, she was startled to see a dark shape on her doorstep. She stopped abruptly, looking at the cloaked figure.

"Hello?"

He turned around. Reg saw with relief that it was just Damon. Still, she wasn't expecting him and was a little unsettled to find him there. She didn't get any closer, but watched him warily, trying to analyze his body language and figure out why he was there without her.

"I just thought I'd drop by to see how you are doing," Damon offered. "It's been a little while and I haven't heard from you…"

"Yeah. I've just been busy with other things. I'm supposed to be helping Francesca with the kattakyns, and there's the gnome in the garden, and just… things." She didn't mention Corvin, knowing that Damon already didn't like or trust him, which was appropriate, but why aggravate him further? She hadn't needed

Damon's protection against Corvin; she'd stood her ground quite well all by herself.

Damon smiled. "The gnome in the garden?"

"Well, yes… he's not exactly my responsibility, Sarah is the one who hired him, but since I'm the one he can communicate with telepathically, these things just keep falling on me."

"What things?"

"His brother was in jail, and I helped to get him out, and then he found the key, and I was trying to find out where it came from or what it opens…"

"An actual physical key. Did you have any luck?"

"Not yet, but I haven't had a chance to look around. Sarah didn't know where it came from, and she's lived here for a long time."

"Yes, she has. If the key predates her, it must be pretty old."

Reg walked closer to Damon, starting to relax after the surprise of his unexpected appearance. He wasn't going to do anything to harm her. He was a friend, and she'd previously used him as a bodyguard. He was safe.

He reached out tentatively, offering a hug in greeting. Reg wasn't a hugger by nature, so she was a little stiff, not knowing if she wanted to accept the hug

He kept it brief, probably sensing she found it awkward. "So where were you?"

"Uh—just now?"

"Yes. Where were you coming from?"

"Just… a thing."

"Work?"

Reg nodded. "Yeah. Meeting with a client."

Damon scowled. But it wasn't any of his business where she had been. She had momentarily forgotten he was a diviner and could tell when she was lying. Even a white lie or something unimportant like where she had been. Now he thought that she had something to hide. She just wanted to preserve her privacy.

She didn't want to talk about Corvin and his possible reintegration into society.

"Were you with Hunter?" Damon asked suspiciously.

"No, I wasn't with Corvin." Reg rolled her eyes dramatically. "You know I don't associate with him."

"For someone who doesn't associate with him, you talk to him and meet with him an awful lot."

"That's over now. That was just over the Witch Doctor, and he's gone now, so there's no more reason for us to meet."

"Yeah? So you haven't seen him at all lately?"

"Sure, I've seen him, but that's different than… *seeing* him." Reg caught herself. "What am I doing justifying myself to you, anyway? Who I talk to is my own business."

"It's just that… I thought we could go out again, but if you're seeing Corvin Hunter, then…"

"No, I'm not seeing Corvin. I happen to talk to him now and then. He calls me. He shows up. What am I supposed to do about that?"

"You could tell him to get lost."

"Do you have any idea how many times I've told him to leave me alone? He keeps coming back. It doesn't matter what I say to him. It doesn't matter whether I light him on fire and testify against him before his coven," Reg pointed out. "You've seen. He keeps coming back. So what am I supposed to do?"

"Stop talking to him."

Reg shrugged impatiently. "The guy is being shunned. Who else is he going to talk to? He'll just keep showing up whether I talk to him or not. He hangs around waiting until everyone leaves. He shows up in my yard or on the street."

"Get a restraining order."

"You can't do that without any reason. He's not threatening me or being violent toward me. What am I supposed to do, tell the judge that I'm afraid he'll take away my powers? How do you think that's going to go over? I'll tell you—they'll lock me up. And I don't have any interest in going through that again. I know what

I'm talking about. So why don't you believe I'd get rid of him if I could, and leave it alone?"

"You could go to his coven and ask them to take steps."

Reg thought back to her meeting with Davyn. "Trust me; they're not going to discipline him."

Damon studied her, then eventually nodded. "Okay. Fine. You weren't seeing him and you can't do anything about him coming around here. All the more reason for me to be around. I can send him on his way and make sure he doesn't bother you."

Reg rolled her eyes at Damon thinking he had the power to overcome Corvin anymore. "Like I said, he'll wait until you're gone. He's not stupid. You two really don't get along together, do you? Is that just now, because of me, or do you have a history?"

"We've never gotten along," Damon said brusquely. "Not many people do get along with his kind. It would be like having a tiger for a pet. You don't know if one day he's not going to turn on you. I'm sorry for sounding so…"

"Jealous?" Reg suggested.

"Yeah, I guess it could come across that way. But I'm not trying to be possessive or to assume a relationship that we don't have. I just want to protect you. I'm interested in you; I think we could have a good time together and enjoy each other's company. Maybe develop into something closer. But with him always hanging on the periphery… it makes me edgy. I don't know what to expect from him. Or from you."

"You know I don't want to get together with him; that's why I asked for your help before."

"That's also why I worry about you being off with him. He could still charm you. Catch you unaware, like before."

"I know what I'm doing now. Or at least, I know what he's trying to do, and I'm getting better at resisting him."

"I just hope… I don't want anything to happen to you."

Reg felt a warm flush. She appreciated both the sentiment and the warmth in his voice. She could see herself getting together with Damon. Their first date hadn't turned out so well, but he had a good heart. They'd nearly lost him in the fight with the Witch Doctor. He'd been badly hurt before Corvin had helped to heal him. But the two of them could find things in common. She and Damon could spend time with each other and enjoy each other's company. She closed her eyes for a moment and pictured the two of them taking in a movie, his arm around her shoulders, sharing a bag of popcorn, relaxed and happy…

"Stop it," she growled, opening her eyes, pushing the vision away from her as hard as she could.

"What?" Damon's brows lifted, but he was not very convincing. He knew exactly what she was talking about.

"Quit putting visions in my head. I don't want you forcing your ideas on me."

"I'm not forcing you. You're just thinking about the possibilities. There's not any coercion involved."

"I can come up with my own ideas. I don't need you putting them into my head."

"How is it any different than listening to spirits or communicating with your gnome? It's just a different mode of communication. I'm just painting a picture."

Reg couldn't put her finger on how it was any different from the way that Forst communicated with her. Damon's pictures were so rich that she wasn't always sure whether what she was seeing was really happening or not, and that was scary. At least with the gnome, it was still words, just on a different level—his inside words instead of his outside words.

"Just stop doing it… or tell me before you do it, or something. I don't like being fooled."

Damon frowned, but he didn't argue. He turned his back to her and reached into her mailbox. Reg tensed warily, not sure what he was doing. Was he putting some spell on it?

But he pulled a small envelope out instead. "I, er, left you a note," he said, his face getting pink. "I didn't know how long it was going to be before you were back."

Used to modern technology, Reg didn't know when the last

time someone had sent her a handwritten note or letter was. She probably would never even have thought to look in the mailbox. Sarah received all of the postal mail at the big house and, rather than leaving it in Reg's mailbox, she always brought it in and left it sorted on the counter for her.

There was a card caught on the envelope of Damon's letter. He pulled them apart and looked at the card. His mouth twisted.

"Davyn Smithy. What was he doing here?"

Reg was confused. Why would Davyn have left a card in her mailbox when she was meeting with him at his office? It didn't make any sense.

Then she remembered what seemed like ages ago. She had refused to let him into the cottage or to take the card from him, worried that he might have laid a curse on it. So he had left it in her mailbox instead, and it had been there ever since.

"Uh… that's from a long time ago. When he was here to tell me about Corvin's hearing."

He examined it more closely and peeked into her mailbox to see if there was anything else incriminating. But being a diviner, he must know that she was telling the truth. He hesitated, not sure what to do with his note or with the business card.

"Just give them to me," Reg said, motioning impatiently.

"But I already talked to you, so I don't need to leave a note… and you don't need the card anymore."

"Give them to me."

Damon handed them to her. The envelope was stiff, not just a note on a piece of paper, but a card. Reg ripped the sealed envelope open. The front was a picture of a tuxedo cat sitting in a window beside some pink flowers in a vase. There was a brief note jotted inside that Reg would sort out later, when she could take the time to figure out the cursive writing.

She was floored that Damon would go to the effort not just to write her a note, but to get a card with a cat like Starlight on the front. He'd planned ahead; he hadn't just pulled a random piece of paper out of his pocket.

"Damon… this is really sweet. Thank you."

"I just wanted you to know that I was thinking about you. I hope everything has been okay since the big fight… I know it wasn't easy for you to face the Witch Doctor, and you were really strong."

"Well, nothing like you," Reg pointed out, embarrassed that she hadn't even asked after his health, let alone his mental and emotional state. The guy had basically been blown up and had nearly died. She could have at least checked in on him. "How are you doing now… everything healing okay?"

"I might not like Hunter, but he did a good job healing me. I haven't had any problems. You wouldn't know that anything had happened."

"Would you… like to come in?"

She hadn't been planning to invite him in. She knew it was a risky thing. If she allowed him into the cottage, then the wards that Sarah had set to protect Reg wouldn't work against him. But he wasn't planning to do anything that would harm her. He had just given her a mushy note.

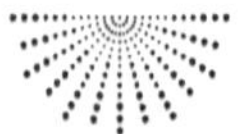

*D*amon's face lit up. No need to study him to read his emotions. "Sure, if you're not busy."

"I don't know what kind of a mess things might be in here; I didn't pay much attention when I left earlier. And I do have to get back to business before too long. But there's no reason we can't visit for a few minutes."

She stood close to him to unlock the door and let him in, her heart racing with his proximity. But she didn't know if it was excitement or anxiety. She followed him into the cottage, reaching out to sense the atmosphere of the room to discern whether she had made a mistake by letting him in. But nothing felt any different. She didn't feel a spell breaking or darkness seeping into the room. It felt just the same as always.

"Have a seat." Reg gestured to the couch. She didn't normally entertain men there and it occurred to her that there wasn't anywhere that would be very comfortable for him to sit. She always found the wicker furniture to be bumpy and pokey, even if it was upholstered. Somehow she always ended up with something sticking into her. She didn't worry about it with her clients, because they were only there for a short session. She didn't want them to get too comfortable and stay on after she had finished with them. "Sorry…"

Damon sat down, easing into the wicker as if he were afraid it would collapse right under him. It didn't break, sag, or creak, so he relaxed his posture.

"Something to drink?" Reg offered. "There's Jack Daniels."

"Sure, that sounds good. I thought you were more of a tea drinker."

"I guess I have been since I got here. You can't exactly drink whiskey all day with clients. But you can have tea; it doesn't hurt anything."

"Jack sounds just fine."

Reg went to pour it and wondered fleetingly if it were too early in the day to start drinking or to be getting friendly with Damon. She didn't want Sarah barging in and making a fuss. She didn't think she had any appointments with clients. Reg flipped the page in her appointment book to make sure and detoured to the front door to lock it before joining Damon. It wouldn't keep Sarah out. She did, after all, have a key, but they would at least have a warning that she was at the door.

She had a key.

Reg put the two glasses down on the coffee table and felt the pocket of her skirt. The old key was still there. Still tugging at her, telling her to find the lock and claim the treasure.

"What's that?" Damon asked, noticing her action.

"Oh…" Reg pulled the key and out displayed it. "Just an old key." She sat down on the couch a comfortable distance away from him.

He looked at it and raised his brows. "Not in very good shape, is it?"

"That's what happens when you bury it in the garden."

"Why would you do that?"

"I didn't. But somebody did."

"Why bother? It doesn't look like anything important."

"It's magical. I don't know what it opens, but I think it could be…" she trailed off, not wanting to speculate on a treasure. What if he wanted a stake or spread the news to others? She wanted whatever the key opened all to herself. "You're probably right. It's probably nothing. Whatever it unlocks probably doesn't even exist anymore. Someone lost the key, so they would have to rekey the lock, and now it's worthless. Someone just lost it in the dark some night."

"Could be," Damon agreed. "There are a lot of keys in the world, and a lot of them get lost."

Reg warmed it between her hands. "I think it looks cool. That's all. You've probably seen tons of old keys in your life. They're probably all over the place here."

"I've seen my share," Damon agreed. "Every house in Black Sands probably has old chests and cupboards that took old style keys. And the keys get put in a drawer somewhere and forgotten about. People tend to collect them, thinking that they'll remember what a key was for or that it was important, and in the end just end up with a drawer full of orphan keys."

Reg sipped her drink. It felt good after the meeting with Davyn. She hadn't noticed how much tension she had been carrying in her shoulders since their meeting. The thought of them commuting Corvin's sentence was deplorable. She hated it. But she didn't have to think about it. She was having a pleasant visit with Damon. She didn't have to think about Corvin or Davyn or anyone else.

Damon also took a drink and gazed at her over the rim of the glass, contemplative. "So what does Reg Rawlins want out of life? Tell me about your hopes and dreams."

That was a tall order. Reg thought about what she could tell him.

But a voice whispered in her ear that she should not answer. Not her subconsciousness. An actual voice that she recognized. She closed her eyes so that Damon wouldn't see her rolling them, and she focused on building a wall around herself. A barrier between her and the irritating voice. It didn't work. She had blocked Norma Jean out for a long time, but since she had come to the surface when Corvin had held Reg's powers, Norma Jean popped up at the most inconvenient junctures. Reg focused on the present. Norma Jean belonged in the past. She was dead. She didn't need to follow Reg around, trying to look after her little girl. That hadn't worked before, and Reg couldn't see it working now.

"Those must be some dreams," Damon teased.

Reg opened her eyes again. "Oh… I don't know. What about you? What are your big dreams?"

"Well… I'd like to find a way to use my powers to make a full-time living. Right now, I do private security, but I really would like to use my talents full time. Not to have to resort to other ways to earn a living."

Reg nodded. "That sounds good."

"I admire you for starting up your own business and jumping in with both feet. There aren't a lot of people who can make good money using magical powers."

"It's not the first time I've done it… and it doesn't usually work out in the end. But maybe this time… things are quite a bit different this time."

"Because of Black Sands?"

"Yeah. I've never had contact with anyone with… real powers before. I didn't even know that's what I had. So to be somewhere like this… it's different."

"And the competition doesn't bother you? Knowing that there are other psychics out there who also have real powers?"

"It's been okay so far. People seem to stick with one practitioner for a while… so I get multiple jobs from one client… I guess sooner or later they'll decide they want to hear something else, and they'll seek out one of the other psychics or mediums."

"There's enough work to go around?"

"So far, so good. It helps that the rent is so reasonable, and Sarah is always getting me new clients. She's very hooked into the community."

Reg didn't express her fears to him. The fact that sooner or later, everything always went down the toilet. And then... where would she go next? That was why she needed the treasure.

"What did you do before you came to Black Sands? Were you doing readings there? Wherever you came from?"

Reg considered the question from several angles before answering. It was better not to answer him than it was to try to lie to him. She wanted to make sure that there was nothing he could use against her in her answer. Corvin had asked her about her past too, and then he had ended up investigating her behind her back, coming up with information that she had regretted him having. She didn't want to repeat the same mistakes.

"Yeah," she agreed. She'd already told him it wasn't the first time she had tried that gig, so by extension he already knew the answer to his question. "I've done readings different times, different places. Mostly just for enough change to get a meal, when I was down on the skids. And..." She decided to stop there. Nothing that would lead him back to Erin and Tennessee. Nothing that would give her away. "Like I say, I've tried it before."

"You didn't have any other practitioners in your family that you know of? Sometimes people don't even realize they have powers."

"It was just me and my mom, for the first few years. Then foster care. I didn't know anyone else in my family. My mom never said that there was anyone with powers. I think she would have said something if they had. If nothing else, she would have been trying to get something from them."

He raised an eyebrow. "Not very complimentary about your mother."

"There's not much I can say about her. She died when I was little. But what I remember... she wasn't the kind of mom on Hallmark commercials."

"Few of them are. But with the powers you have, you must have someone in your family. It doesn't usually come out of nowhere."

"No."

"You don't know anything about your father?"

Norma Jean was setting up a ruckus in Reg's head. She narrowed her eyes, trying to keep her focus on Damon rather than her mother's rampaging spirit. Was he fishing? Did he know something? She wasn't sure how much of her conversation with the Witch Doctor had been out loud and how much had been inside her head. Had the others heard? She was still trying to figure everything out herself. Hints dropped by the Witch Doctor, Harrison, and Norma Jean.

"No, nothing at all."

He clearly knew that was false. Reg cursed herself for not being able to lie to him convincingly. She was so used to changing the truth to suit her needs. Most people couldn't tell when she was lying. It was habitual, even though she knew that Damon would be able to recognize the truth when he heard it—or didn't.

"Look," she said, "this is none of your business. I don't want to talk about the past or my family. You don't know what it was like growing up the way I did. It's something I'd rather forget. We can… talk about your childhood or dreams. I don't like to."

He stretched his arm out behind her. He brushed the back of her hair, setting her thin red braids swaying. "You don't see a lot of redheads with cornrows."

His touch was comfortable. She didn't feel any anxiety over it. But on the other hand, she didn't feel the magnetism toward him that she felt toward Corvin, either. Was she going to compare everyone to Corvin now? She hated her magical attraction to him. Why did she have to react to his charms? Even when he wasn't there to magick her, she was still thinking about how amazing it felt to be with him. Would it never go away?

"Reg?"

She refocused on Damon. "Hmm?"

"Where did you get them done? It must have taken a long time."

"Oh, the braids. Yeah. Hours. But then I don't have to do

much to take care of them." She fingered them, feeling down the tight bumps of one braid. "I'll have to get them redone before too long. I wonder if there is anyone here who does it."

"Bound to be someone. If not, you could go with dreadlocks like the Witch Doctor."

Reg shuddered. "I don't think I'm going to do that."

"You think the Witch Doctor was really the one who killed your mother? He wasn't just manipulating you to think that?"

"Well, I still remember the same things, so… yeah. I do. I wish I could remember more… and I wish I couldn't remember anything. It was better when I didn't remember any of it."

"Even though you didn't remember, it probably still affected you. Seeing something like that can cause a lot of psychological damage."

"It wasn't an easy childhood. I'm glad to be an adult now, independent. I was never really comfortable living in a family. Never fit in." She laughed. "How would I? Try fitting a traumatized kid with the ability to see ghosts into any home."

Damon smiled. "You're right. That would be pretty tough, unless everyone knew what they were getting."

Reg nodded. She looked away from him, trying to think of the best way to get back off the topic and to focus the conversation on him instead.

"And what about Harrison," Damon said slowly, "you don't think he's your father?"

"Harrison?" Reg shook her head; her forehead creased into worry lines that made it ache. "No, of course not. How could he be? These immortals, whatever they are, they wouldn't have anything to do with humans."

"I'm not so sure. There are plenty of stories about mortal women and immortal men."

"Mythology. That stuff isn't real."

"That's not what you said when we were fighting the Witch Doctor."

"I was trying to distract him. That was our job, remember? I didn't say I believed it. I was just trying to get a rise out of him."

"I see." His eyes were steady, burning into her. Seeing right through everything she tried to tell him. "So. Not Harrison. Then who?"

"No one. I told you. Some client or scummy boyfriend. Someone she'd never met before. A nobody. Street dirt."

"If you didn't get your powers through your mother's family, then you must have gotten them through your father's."

"Or they were just spontaneous. Or acquired some other way. I don't know. There are other ways, aren't there?"

"Yes, but they are very rare."

"So I'm a rare case."

"You certainly are," he agreed with a warm smile.

"Can we stop talking about my family? It's… depressing."

And she hoped that if they stopped talking about it, Norma Jean's voice in her head would stop screeching. She was getting a nasty headache.

She took another sip of her drink.

Reg heard Starlight jump down off the bed or the windowsill and, in a moment, he walked into sight and approached Reg. He sniffed in Damon's direction, watching the man suspiciously. Reg watched to see how Damon would react to Starlight. Corvin hated him. Harrison loved him. Reg thought that was a pretty good barometer of what kind of people they were. Damon smiled politely and reached his fingers down, holding them out for Starlight to smell. After ignoring his fingers for a few moments, Starlight decided to check them out. He sniffed Damon's hand thoroughly, then rubbed against it. Damon obligingly gave his ears and chin a few scratches, then sat back up.

"We always had cats around growing up."

"Were they familiars?"

"No, just house pets. They might have given my mother a little magical support; I don't know. She never said so. And they weren't treated like..." he searched for the words. "They weren't treated as equals. They were pets."

Reg nodded. Starlight wandered away to look at his dish. Altogether, the interaction between Damon and Starlight had been a non-event. So maybe that told her what she needed to know about him. He was just in the middle. Not great, not evil or dangerous, just a typical, everyday kind of guy. Other than the fact that he did have some magical powers. Reg was getting accustomed to the fact that everyone in Black Sands seemed to have something or other. She didn't ask what they were or what they could do, just trying to stay open-minded towards new people until she learned their quirks.

"Did you ever have a familiar? I thought it was pretty common, but I guess maybe not. Corvin doesn't like animals."

"That's probably because he is one. He doesn't like the competition." Damon snickered.

Reg wasn't sure how she felt about Corvin, but she didn't like making fun of him behind his back. She didn't join in Damon's laughter.

She had been moving the key from one hand to the other as they talked, absently fidgeting with it. She felt the now-familiar tug to unlock the treasure. She needed to know what it fit and she needed to open it. Was there an attic in the cottage? She didn't think so, but there were lots of rooms and, she was sure, an attic too in Sarah's house. Maybe Sarah wouldn't mind Reg going through the house to see if she could find the lock that the key belonged to and reunite them.

She could see herself fitting the key into the lock. Feel it turning in her hand, clicking into place just as it should with a satisfying click, and then the tumbler turning and revealing to her the priceless treasure within...

"Are you doing that?" she demanded.

Damon raised his eyebrows. "Doing what?"

"I told you not to put thoughts into my head. Were you just doing that with the key?"

He shook his head, looking baffled. If he were lying, she couldn't tell. It wasn't very fair that he could lie to her, but she couldn't lie to him. It should work both directions. "No. What do you mean? What about the key?"

"I just... never mind. I don't know what I'm thinking. I'm tired. I shouldn't be drinking."

He took the glass out of her hand and downed what remained in one gulp, then put it down on the coffee table with a grin. "There. Problem solved."

Reg stared at him in shock for a moment, then burst into laughter. He was right; one problem solved. And such an easy solution. She should put the key away too. If it were going to be that distracting for her, she should just let it go and forget about it for a while. She would search for the lock later. She didn't want to lose it, fiddling with it absently. Who knew where she might put it down in a moment of distraction.

But the key was warm in her hand and she didn't want to put it back in her pocket.

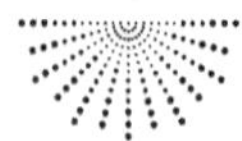

After Damon went home, Reg decided to focus on work. She got out her computer and worked on a marketing plan, wrote down the things she would need to do, who she should contact, what supplies she needed. But all the while, she was distracted by the key. The key would be better than a marketing plan. Because no matter how hard she worked on the marketing plan, there would always be more to do. She would never be able to forget about it and let the business run itself. That wasn't the way that it worked. But if she used the key to unlock the treasure, then she wouldn't have to worry about it again. She would be set for life. She would have all of the wealth she needed to live the way she wanted to.

That was way better than a marketing plan.

Reg decided to leave the computer alone and do something about finding the treasure. That would be much more productive.

She closed the lid of her laptop and went outside to the garden to look around. If the key had been found there, then why not the lock?

The garden was deserted. It was definitely looking better. She didn't usually see Forst working in it, but he obviously had been. A large portion of the plants had been beaten flat before and were now standing up on their own. A few were staked and tied, but most of them seemed to have sprung back up on their own. Birds were singing in the trees. It was very peaceful and calm.

"It is a happier place," Forst said.

Reg startled and looked around. He was standing just a few feet away from her, but she had failed to see him or to hear his approach.

"You scared me! Where did you come from?"

"Gnomen are like humans. The babies grow in the mother's womb. But Gnomen always have two kinder. And very rare to have more than one set."

"Uh… I didn't mean where do gnome babies come from. I mean, where were you just now? I didn't see you here and I didn't hear you come."

"I was in the soil."

Reg considered this, but she wasn't sure what he meant. Rather than look like a fool asking another fundamental question, she just shook it off. Forst was looking happy, his cheeks a glowing red. His overalls were grubby, but he looked like he'd been having a good time. Gardening certainly agreed with him.

"How is Fir? Is everything all right with him?"

Forst nodded vigorously. "He is still in his garden. No more black coats have taken him away. The living are protected, thanks to Reg Rawlins."

"Good. Glad to hear it." She didn't often do something just for others. She recognized that like Corvin, she wasn't altruistic. When she did a thing, it was because she expected to get something out of it. She liked to help others, but that was secondary to her goals. She had been on the streets enough to know that she had to take care of herself first. No one else was going to do that. But helping Fir hadn't been for her. It hadn't been done with any expectation that it would bring her something.

It had made Forst happy, and it was Forst who had found the key, so in a way, it had ended up benefiting her anyway. Life was strange sometimes.

She had the key in her pocket and wrapped her hand around it as she contemplated Forst.

"I'm looking for the lock for the key you found. Do you know anything about… where it is or what kind of a lock it would be?"

He shook his head. "The garden is happier without it. See how well it grows now. Even the birds sing more sweet."

"I thought that the lock might be somewhere close by." Reg looked around for inspiration. "A garden shed or a storage trunk. What do you think?"

"It was a key," Forst said with a shrug. "It opens something."

"Yes. I know. That's what I'm looking for. What do you think it unlocks?"

With his thumbs in his pockets and his belly sticking out, Forst shook his head. "Beware of what a dark key may unlock."

"A dark key?"

He patted his pockets for his pipe and lit it before answering. The smoke wafted lazily through the air. Reg raised her eyebrows, waiting for him to answer the question. "The key made the garden dark. The living plants did not want to grow strong while it was here. It was a dark key."

"But you don't know what it opens. You haven't seen one like that before, or seen anything around here that is locked that it might fit?"

He shook his head and puffed on the pipe. "I have seen no lock it might fit."

"And you don't know what kind of a lock it would be?"

He tapped on the side of the bowl. "It is an old key. It had been in the ground almost as long as you have been alive. Who would bury a key in this garden?"

"It's not that old, if it's only as old as me. There must be all kinds of houses around here that are a hundred years old or more. This looks much older than me."

"The key is older than you." His tone took on a note of impatience. "And it has been in the ground almost as long as you have been alive."

"Oh. But before that, it was somewhere else. It was lost thirty years ago."

"It was never lost."

"But it was lost in the garden," Reg pointed out. "Someone walking through here must have dropped it by accident and never found it."

"No. It was not lost."

Reg left Forst smoking, not sure what to make of this. She made a circuit around the garden, looking at the plants and flowers, but what she wanted to find was a treasure chest or storage shed she could fit the key into. She hadn't explored the back yard before; she usually just walked from the front where she parked her car, along the sidewalk, and into her cottage. She hadn't paid much attention to anything else in the yard.

There were trees, the garden, a birdbath with water in it, and a bench to sit on and take it all in.

But no storage shed. No trunk. Nothing that required a key.

* * *

When Reg awoke in the morning, she could feel Starlight sitting on the bed close to her leg. Normally, he was either looking out the window or poking at her face trying to wake her up. Maybe he was looking for some cuddle time. She reached out to pet him, but the form she touched was not a furry cat.

Her eyes flew open and she practically leapt out of her bed. It was not a cat sitting on the edge of the bed beside her, but a man. Before she had even had a chance to recognize him, her brain had already processed several possibilities. Corvin's powers had become great enough for him to break any of the simple wards that Sarah had placed there against him. She had allowed Damon in, and that meant that he was allowed to come back, recognized as a guest rather than an intruder. Or it was a burglar or some other stranger there to harm her.

Then as she clambered out of bed, her eyes caught up with her brain and she realized that it was Harrison.

The long-limbed, smiling man looked at her curiously.

As usual, he was dressed in a style that just missed looking like a modern Floridian. He had on a long-sleeved white shirt with puffy sleeves, like he was a pirate or an English lord of some bygone era. This was paired with long, narrow-legged gray pants with pinstripes. He did seem to like his stripes. He had an enormous, dramatic mustache, and while she stared at him, he twirled the ends, making sure that they were properly styled.

"You are... what are you doing in my house?" she demanded. "You scared the heck out of me. You can't just walk into other people's houses like that."

"I didn't walk in."

"Well, you can't apparate or whatever it was you did. You are supposed to call or knock and get permission before going into someone's house. And how is it you can just appear here? I thought Sarah put up wards against unwelcome intruders."

He shrugged. He got up from the bed and bent at the window to pick up Starlight, who immediately started purring. The traitor. He should have been supporting Reg by telling Harrison that he couldn't just appear in the cottage without warning.

Harrison walked with Starlight out toward the kitchen. Reg followed, not sure what else to do.

"I haven't seen you for a while. What have you been doing?" she asked him.

He put Starlight down and poked at the coffee machine as if trying to prod an animal into action. Reg walked over, added grounds, and pushed the button to start it working. Harrison's eyes lit up, and he smiled and nodded.

"Ingenious!"

"Yeah. Coffee machine. Pretty state-of-the-art. You haven't answered my questions. What are you doing here? Where have you been? I thought we would see you after the fight with the Witch Doctor. I thought you would appear, tell us what a good job we did… I don't know, knight us or something. It was really hard."

"You did very well," he confirmed with a nod. "Destine would have been difficult for anyone to fight, and for a group of mortals to be able to overcome him, that was impressive. You used your assets and accomplished something great."

But he said it without inflection, as if it didn't mean anything to him. What could mere mortals mean to someone like him? He must have had much more important things on his mind. Immortal things.

"What exactly is an immortal?" she asked, watching him as he watched the coffee machine pop and sputter. "Is it a god? An alien race? Where do you come from?"

Harrison glanced over at her. He looked down at Starlight as if he might have the answer to the question, then opened the fridge to find something to feed Starlight. As if Reg couldn't feed her own cat. But she knew how much Harrison loved cats and couldn't find fault with him for that.

"It is the best word we could find in your language," he said, "but it is rather inadequate. There is so much more to my kind than simply living longer than human memory. But it is the best we can do."

"Are you immortal? Un-killable?"

"Death is an interesting human concept." He found a bowl of spicy chicken Reg had brought home from The Crystal Bowl a few days previous. He started to shred it for Starlight.

"That might bother his stomach," Reg pointed out.

Harrison looked at Starlight, who stared at him, communicating something, then Harrison continued to shred the chicken. "Humans call it death, and yet they talk of life after death. They know that death is not the end of the spirit, that consciousness goes on somewhere else or in a new life, but they still believe it is permanent." He shrugged as if it were impossible to comprehend such convoluted logic.

Reg had to admit that despite her dedicated non-belief in any mainstream religion or the concept of heaven or reincarnation, she knew that spirits lived on after the death of the body. How else had Norma Jean continued to talk to Reg long after her death? And so many other spirits that Reg had communicated with over the years. The only other way to explain it would be to admit that she was insane and that the voices and visions were just a glitch in her brain, not something that was real and could be explained spiritually.

"And the immortals? How are they different from humans, other than having stronger magical powers?"

"Better fashion sense," Harrison deadpanned.

He bent down and put the chicken in Starlight's bowl. Starlight immediately charged in, chawing on the food noisily as if he hadn't been fed in a week. Reg shook her head. "I need to use the bathroom. Are you going to be here still when I get out?"

"I expect I will."

Reg wasn't sure what that meant, but it was probably as clear as Harrison was going to get. "And you understand the part about privacy and not walking in on people or apparating in the room when they are using the bathroom?"

He cast his eyes down like a child caught with his hand in the cookie jar. "I will not appear in the bathroom."

"Good."

She made quick use of the bathroom in spite of his assurance, not trusting that he would be true to his word. She splashed water on her face and inched the curtain back to peek out the window. It was still early, but it was, at least, light outside. He hadn't gotten her up in the middle of the night. But just how long had he been sitting on her bed before she had awakened?

She returned to the kitchen. The coffee maker was just finished filling the pot, so she poured a cup for herself and one for Harrison. She handed it to him, but he didn't take it.

"I don't drink coffee."

"Then why did you want to make coffee?" Reg demanded, exasperated.

"You drink coffee."

"You were just making it for me?"

"Yes."

"Oh." She sipped her coffee, a little mollified. "Well, thank you for thinking of me. Do you want to sit down?" she motioned to the wicker furniture.

He surveyed it for a moment, then nodded, and they both went over to sit. Starlight had finished eating his chicken and followed them over. Rather than joining Reg, he jumped up onto Harrison's lap, where he received plenty of scratches and snuggles. Reg shook her head at the black hairs collecting on Harrison's white pirate shirt.

"You have questions for me," Harrison said abruptly.

Reg tried to avoid rolling her eyes. "I have plenty of questions, but you never seem to answer any of them. You give some vague answer or change the subject."

"What do you want to know?"

Reg tried to prioritize her questions, suspecting that he would only answer one or two—if she were lucky.

"Who is—or was—Weston?"

He looked at her for a long moment, and she figured he regretted his offer to answer her questions. "Weston is an immortal."

"I figured that. Is he still…" She hesitated over her wording. Asking whether he was alive or dead would likely result in another philosophical discussion over the meaning of the words. "Is he still here, on the earth, like you are?"

"On the earth… not like me." Harrison considered, then nodded, looking satisfied with his answer.

It might have made perfect sense to him, but it didn't tell Reg any more than she already knew.

"He's on the earth right now."

"Yes." He looked as if he would qualify his answer, then shrugged. Reg analyzed his hesitation. Could Weston be on the earth but not on the earth? Maybe, like the pixies, he existed in more than one plane, so that it wasn't as easy to state what temporal space he occupied. If he even had a physical body. The Witch Doctor and Harrison seemed to be able to materialize at will, and she didn't know what happened to their bodies when they weren't visible. Did they occupy only one space? What happened to the matter that made up their bodies when they were not there?

"How is he not here like you?"

"He is… constrained. Not free to come and go."

"Okay…" That was interesting. "Why did the Witch Doctor want to know where he is? And what does he have to do with me or my mother?"

Harrison petted Starlight and looked down at his face. They seemed to be communicating at a telepathic level, but Reg couldn't hear whatever it was they were saying. She didn't like the isolation she felt at not being in on the conversation. It was strange to think that that was how other people felt all the time when she communicated with spirits or telepaths.

"Weston and Destine have been rivals for a very long time. This is not a bad thing in our kind. It creates balance. Keeps one entity from becoming too powerful."

"But you also said that you are prohibited from harming each other. The Witch Doctor definitely wanted to harm Weston. Even to destroy him."

Harrison shrugged. "Rules are broken… if we did not have the freedom to break them, they would not be rules. They would be…" he struggled to find the words, "impossibility. But it is not impossible for us to hurt our kind. That is why there must be a rule."

Reg tried to follow the logic but wasn't sure she did. "And my mother?"

"It is not against the rules to harm mortals."

Reg didn't like to hear that, but it wasn't what she meant. "I mean… how was she involved in all of this? She wasn't immortal."

"No," Harrison laughed, "certainly not." He looked down at

Starlight and stopped laughing as if he had been reprimanded. "No. But she was a favorite. He gave her his blood."

Reg pictured some cannibalistic ritual and wrinkled her nose. "Gave her his blood? What does that mean? Did that… give her power?"

"No." Harrison met Reg's eyes, his golden brown irises glowing. "He gave her you."

CHAPTER FOURTEEN

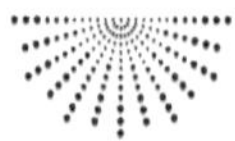

*E*ven though Reg had half-expected this ever since the confrontation with the Witch Doctor, it still sent her reeling. She was suddenly lightheaded, bright spots appearing before her eyes. She didn't want to misunderstand Harrison's use of the English language. Things didn't always come out the way he intended them. She could be completely misunderstanding him. Maybe he meant that Weston had protected her at some point. That she had run away or been kidnapped, and he had brought her back. Or that he'd healed her from a potentially fatal illness.

He had given Reg to Norma Jean.

"He was a man," Norma Jean said in Reg's head. "Just a man like any other. He didn't seem that different."

But he had been, hadn't he?

"Do you mean… that he's my biological father?" Reg asked Harrison as calmly as she could.

Harrison scratched his head. "Biological… I am not sure. My kind… it is not the same as when humans meet. But without him, you were not. And with him, you were."

Reg groaned. She brought her feet up onto the chair, knees tight against her chest. "Don't tell me that! Then these… gifts that I have? They are from him?"

"They are… part of him." Harrison pondered. "We don't know when we create with a human, what will be the result. A child with great powers, or a child with little power at all. When a child is born, there is… a disruption in our order. We can sense it… That is how I knew of your existence and your need for protection."

"But why would you protect me? If Weston was my father, then wasn't it *his* responsibility?"

"He was… gathered in. There is a consequence to creation. He could not be there. But he left no clues to his chosen exile."

"So the Witch Doctor couldn't find him."

"Destine would have if he could. We are vulnerable when in that state. Destine hoped to remove him from this earth. The rest of us watched for him, but Destine was more… dedicated."

"And he thought Norma Jean would know where Weston went? That he would leave her a trail of breadcrumbs so she could find him again?"

"Breadcrumbs." His face lit up with a big smile. "What an apt word. For Weston to come back, he would need to be close to his loved one. But Destine was unable to find the trail. He was furious. And he has been searching still, waiting for some sign of Weston's return."

Reg shook her head. "And I walked right into him. What are the odds that I would move into the town he was operating out of?"

"Odds?"

"What are the chances that we would run into each other? I managed to lose him all those years ago in Maine. We should never have run into each other again. But then I decide to come to Black Sands because it sounded like a good place to run a con as a psychic. And things would never be the same again…"

"It is not chance," Harrison said slowly. "It was certainty. You and Destine were both drawn to this place."

"Why?"

He raised his eyebrows comically high. "Because Weston was

here. He left his imprint on the place. It is very faint, so many years later, but not so faint that one of our kind cannot feel it."

"And me? Do you think I could sense him here too?"

Harrison nodded. "Why else would you come here? Traveling all across the country? Humans like to stay in one place, near their nesting place. They don't like to go long temporal distances. But you did not stay. You came here when you had no one to help take care of you, no job, no roots. Just... Weston's imprint."

"I don't know." Reg shook her head. "I know why I came here, and it wasn't just a feeling that I should. It was a decision based on logic. On trying to earn money to support myself."

"Humans can work anywhere. You did not have to come to this location to work."

"Well, no," Reg agreed. "I have worked in other places, and I move fairly often. But Black Sands seemed like a good place to land. I heard that there were more witches and psychics here than anywhere else in the country. So, of course, I came here."

Harrison nodded and petted Starlight with long, slow strokes.

"This is crazy. Everyone keeps asking me where I got my talents. And I thought... they were just something I developed to survive. Learning to cold read people. To avoid trouble. How to know when people were telling the truth, and whether they were a danger to me. I needed those things to survive. I didn't even know there was such a thing as a real psychic gift until I moved here. And even now, I don't understand it and half the time don't even believe it myself."

"We have observed that humans who go through hardship develop stronger gifts. Or humans with stronger gifts run into more problems. We don't know why this is. In some cultures, children are taken away from their families, are put through trials, in order to force the development of their inborn talents."

Reg remembered Calliopia's kidnapping and incarceration with the pixies. She remembered Calliopia's father talking about the ordeal she had been through. Reg had suspected at the time that he had been the one to put her through it, but she couldn't understand why he would do such a thing. Maybe it had been to force the development of her fairy gifts, to trick her into coming into her powers.

"That's cruel. I know what it's like to have to live without parents. No one should ever do that."

Harrison shrugged as if it were nothing. According to Francesca, immortals didn't have any feelings for humans, but saw them just as bugs or amusing toys, to play with and discard as they liked. Harrison had been helpful to Reg, and she had good feelings around him, but did he love her like the uncle he had once pretended to be? Did he care how she felt or how she turned out in life? Or was he part of the reason she had gone through so many difficulties, carefully nudging her gifts to blossom, like someone forcing flower bulbs?

Harrison's eyes roved around the room.

"Why are you really here?" Reg asked suspiciously. "You didn't come here because you thought I had questions you could answer. You haven't ever cared about my questions before. You always avoid answering them."

Harrison gave her a cheerful smile, a mask that covered up whatever his real motives were. He wasn't easy for her to read, especially since he could block her psychic powers. "Perhaps I wanted to see my old friend again," he offered, indicating Starlight. He kissed the top of the cat's head and cuddled him close to his face. Reg found it very uncomfortable to see him doting on a cat like a little child or crazy cat lady. It was nice that he liked cats, but he seemed to like them just a little too much.

"Do you want a cat? We have nine that we are trying to find new homes for."

He chuckled. "It would not be a good choice for me to provide a temporal home for another creature. Especially a kattakyn."

Reg watched him as he continued to lavish attention on Starlight. "Did you… know him in another life? Or when he was with another owner?" She had taken his 'old friend' as a tongue-in-cheek joke, but maybe it had been accurate. Perhaps he had known Starlight for longer than she thought. They had acted immediately comfortable and friendly with each other from the first time they met.

Harrison looked into Starlight's face for a moment. "He is a very old, wise soul."

"So you do know him?"

Reg picked up her coffee cup and sipped the cooling liquid. She really ought to have something to eat before all of the caffeine gave her the shakes. When she looked back at Harrison for his answer to her question, he was no longer there.

* * *

Reg spent what felt like hours on the phone with the people at the animal shelter, being passed from one person to another, trying to find out what they knew about Starlight's history and his previous owner. She would not have been at all surprised to learn that his previous owner had been named Harrison, or some other familiar name. Just how many people had lied to her about the cat's history? Did anyone at the shelter know that he was psychic? That he was an ancient soul? Reg didn't even know what that meant, but she felt embarrassed that she had always just treated him like a cat when he seemed to be something more, at least when Harrison talked about him. Corvin had once suggested that Starlight might be a reincarnate, a cat that had been a person in a previous life. But Reg didn't believe in rein-carnation.

Just like she didn't believe in ghosts or magic. How far had that gotten her?

She remembered the worker at the shelter telling her that Starlight's previous owner had died, and that was why he had been so depressed and not responded to anyone until Reg's arrival. He had connected to her like he hadn't to anyone else. Was that some-thing to do with Harrison? Maybe Reg had been predestined to go to Black Sands and maybe she was supposed to get a cat and be a psychic and whatever else Weston had declared.

She was angry whenever she thought of Weston. Why would he bring a child into the world when it was against their rules and she was bound to live a life of hardship and be on the outside, never belonging? What was the benefit to him? Was he playing with them like pieces on a chess board? Because of what he had done, Norma Jean had been tortured and killed. There had been so many negative consequences; Reg didn't understand why he would risk it. What was the good of bringing a child into such a world?

She put her phone down on the coffee table, watching Starlight, expecting him to start acting like a person or to be transformed into one in front of her eyes. But he acted just like he always did, finding a bright sunbeam and sitting with one hind leg splayed out while he washed. Her phone buzzed. She looked at the screen.

Corvin.

Not phoning her this time, but sending a text message.

How about dinner?

Reg looked at the time and texted him back. *Bit early, isn't it?*

She felt guilty as soon as she sent the text. Her answer should have been a resounding no. Or ignoring him. She shouldn't even consider the proposition. He was too dangerous.

But she wanted to ask him about Starlight and to see what he thought about Harrison's various claims. Was Harrison leading her on? Seeing what kind of imaginary story he could get her to believe?

Corvin was a historian. He would be able to tell her about the immortals, what the rumors and myths were. And he could tell her why he didn't like Starlight, and why Starlight didn't like him. Was the enmity between them more than just that of someone who didn't like cats?

Corvin's return text buzzed. *Early or late, whatever time you like.*

She shouldn't even be able to receive a text from him. Hadn't she blocked him from her phone? He must have either changed his number or somehow magicked her phone to change the settings. Maybe that last time he had been there, waiting on the street for her. He'd said that he knew she had blocked him, something that she didn't think he should be able to tell from his end.

Where? She texted back. *Somewhere with people.*

It hadn't stopped him the last time. He had just charmed her into wanting to go somewhere they could be alone. He had convinced her to do things she swore she would not do. But she was stronger now. She had learned how to block him. Most of the time. She was feeling stronger and more sure of herself. And if she had the magic of an immortal, then she should be able to do anything she set her mind on, shouldn't she?

She was half-expecting him to suggest The Crystal Bowl, since that was where they had met more often than not. He obviously liked it there. And then there was the fancy place that he had taken her the night that he did manage to steal her powers. She wouldn't want to go back there, though the food had been fantastic. With the way that he had charmed her, she probably would have thought that dirt tasted good.

Harbor Port of Call?

Reg hadn't been there before. It would, she assumed, be a seafood menu. Which was okay with her.

Okay. Send me address.

I'll pick you up, Corvin texted back.

Reg considered. It would mean he would be coming back to the cottage with her. Would she be able to keep him out?

She was feeling reckless. She was angry at Weston, the Witch Doctor, and even Harrison, feeling betrayed by these immortals who played with human lives. They had affected the course of her life. If she would even have had a life without them in the first place. If Corvin had all of the Witch Doctor's powers, then she wouldn't be able to withstand him anyway, so what was the point of planning every move? If she lost her powers, then maybe she would live a normal life. Maybe she would be able to be a normal person who didn't have to face all of the hardships that had dogged her for her whole life.

Fine. Seven o'clock?

He texted her back a smiley face. Reg was slightly disconcerted. She was used to most of the witches and warlocks she knew eschewing technology, at least to some extent, living as if they had been born a couple of centuries before. She wouldn't even have predicted that Corvin knew how to make a smiley.

She put her phone back down and sat down.

Her heart was pumping hard as if she'd been running. Starlight had been snoozing on the couch next to her. He raised his head and looked at her reproachfully, as if he knew what she had just done. Reg rubbed her nose. "It was going to happen sooner or later anyway," she told him irritably. "I just don't feel like fighting anymore."

* * *

She had the rest of the afternoon and early evening to feel guilty and unsettled, but at the same time, pumped up and excited. She felt like she was doing something proactive instead of just sitting around waiting for magical forces to control her life. She had made at least one decision for herself.

She had no idea how formal the Harbor Port of Call was. She assumed that if it were very formal, Corvin would have told her. She could ask Sarah, but that would mean telling her that she had a date with the warlock she was not supposed to be going out with. It was almost certain to end in disaster.

One of her skirts should do just fine. If it wasn't fancy enough, Corvin could deal with it. They could go to The Crystal Bowl instead.

When seven o'clock finally rolled around, Reg was ready to go. Far from deciding to jam out on Corvin after all, she was eager to get on with it. It was perhaps the stupidest thing she had ever knowingly done in her life, but she felt there was no other way to move forward. She was looking at her phone to check the time when the text from Corvin came in.

I'm here. Coming around to your door and assuming you don't have plans to shoot me.

Reg grinned. That wasn't a bad idea—one way to get rid of him once and for all. Though with the powers he had acquired from the Witch Doctor, she wasn't sure a bullet would be enough to kill him. His ability to heal Damon had been impressive. If he could bring the same powers to bear on his own injuries, it was going to take a lot more than a bullet to kill him.

Come at your own risk, she texted back.

In a couple of minutes, she heard his footsteps on the path and got up. When he reached her door, she opened it. She was all ready to go. She didn't invite him in, but stepped out and pulled the door shut behind her.

Corvin looked down at her, his dark eyes gleaming. "I wasn't expecting this."

"I know. I… wasn't either. But I had to get out and I… want to do something. Not just sit around waiting for something to happen to me."

"That's fine with me."

He touched her arm to escort her to the front of the big house, and Reg thrilled at the buzz like an electrical shock that ran all the way up her arm in a shiver. Corvin smiled. "You are indeed reckless tonight."

Reg nodded. Corvin walked with her out to his car. The big black one, not the little white compact she usually saw him in. Dates dictated the bigger car. He opened and held the door for her. The paint on the vehicle was glistening, looking like it had been hand-detailed, and the interior was freshly shampooed and vacuumed, in pristine condition. Reg slid into her seat and Corvin shut the door gently.

"Have you been to the Port of Call before?" he asked after getting into the driver's seat.

"No. I wasn't sure what kind of a place to expect." Reg appraised Corvin's dress. Dark slacks and black silk shirt with a cloak over the top. "I'm not underdressed?"

He shook his head and pulled the car out into the street. "No, you're just right. As usual."

Reg rolled her eyes at the comment.

"I take it you didn't talk to Sarah about it."

"No, certainly not. I didn't need a lecture."

"Well, I'm delighted you changed your mind. Can I ask… why? I know you said that you wanted to do something; I'm just wondering if something happened to prompt that."

"We'll talk about it over supper. I want to pick your brain."

"That seems only fair."

Reg watched out the window, not wanting to look at him. Since capturing the draugrs, she had not seen any more black cats roaming around Black Sands, but she still kept her eyes open, just in case. Maybe the Witch Doctor had created more and Reg hadn't detected them all. Or perhaps he had an apprentice who knew how to do it. Or he could still operate on some level since the kattakyns were still all together.

CHAPTER FIFTEEN

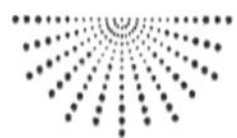

The Harbor Port of Call was a large white house, lots of square corners and windows, the warm light glowing from inside like a fire. Reg stayed put as she was told while Corvin walked around the car to her door and opened it for her. Old style manners. But she wasn't fooled. She knew they were just a veneer over the predatory creature underneath. He dressed up well, but a wolf in sheep's clothing was still a wolf. He escorted her up to the door of the restaurant, and inside the hostess quickly found his reservation and escorted them to a table.

"Is this all right?" Corvin asked, giving Reg the opportunity to approve of or reject it.

It wasn't a private room where they would be all by themselves, but in a busy part of the restaurant, near the bar, where there would be plenty of people coming and going. Witnesses if he tried anything. A good distraction if she wanted to people-watch instead of visiting. He wasn't going to try anything until it was time to go. He would be charming, but not use his magical charms. Maybe just a little to soften her up, but the real attack wouldn't come until later.

"Yes, this is fine."

The hostess nodded, informed them that the waiter would be

coming for their drink order in a moment, and left them alone. Reg picked one of the chairs and sat down so that she could see people coming and going from the bar. And she could also see one of the TVs that hung behind the bar, currently showing a baseball game.

"I assume the thing to get here is the seafood?" Reg questioned, flicking open her menu and looking at the pictures.

"Of course. Very fresh. Swimming until moments before it hits your plate."

Reg felt revulsion at his words. She liked fish and seafood, but she didn't like his cold reference to them being alive. She preferred to ignore the reality that she was eating another creature. Especially after Corvin's talk about how his drinking a person's powers was no different from her eating meat. There was a difference. Wasn't there?

She looked at the salads. Maybe something lighter. She thought about Forst and Fir and their gardens. They loved living things so much. Gnomes were vegetarian. She could anticipate their joy over eating something they had grown themselves. Something they had nurtured from a seed.

"What are you thinking about?" Corvin gazed across the table at her, his mouth curling up slightly.

"Oh… Sarah's garden gnome. I never knew they were a real thing."

"She has a gnome?"

"Well, it's not hers. He's not, I mean. He's working for her, but she doesn't own him. He's helping her with the damage that she did to the garden when she was… not well."

"They are a very ancient race," Corvin said, nodding. "Very… natural. Earthy. Anchored."

"They have…" Reg struggled to find the right words. "They don't seem to have the same prejudices about emotions that humans do. Most of the other races that I've dealt with are quite reserved; they don't show you what they're feeling. But the gnomes are… emotional. Happy or sad, they let you see it. It's very… freeing."

"You feel the need to wear a mask?"

"Doesn't everyone?"

"Some more than others."

"I guess that growing up, I was always told to suck it up. If you have a problem, you deal with it the best you can. You don't complain or tell anyone how hurt or scared you are. Nobody wants to have to deal with your problems."

"That must make it very difficult to ask anyone for help as an adult."

"Yeah. Sure does. Especially since grown-ups are supposed to be able to handle their own problems. You're supposed to be able to do everything for yourself. Make those tough decisions. Be successful. People who can't take care of themselves are… sort of a lower caste. If you're homeless or disabled or mentally ill… then you're vulnerable."

Corvin nodded. "You've had to be very tough. You've been forced to be hard, to be stubborn."

"To look out for myself." Reg remembered what Harrison had said about her gifts causing her hardships, or the hardships bringing out her gifts. Her mouth twisted into a scowl, though she tried to hide it behind the glass of water that the hostess had poured for her. She looked around for the waiter. They should have been able to place their drink orders already.

"Did something happen today?" Corvin asked. "You said we were going to talk about it."

"Harrison." Reg caught the eye of one of the waiters and gestured him over. Corvin waited for her to provide more information, but she was more interested in getting a drink. They each placed their orders, Corvin taking care this time not to offend her by ordering on her behalf, and the smiling waiter promised to be back with them in short order.

Reg sat back, waiting. She wanted something that would help to numb the feelings and calm her anxiety. She really shouldn't have broken down and agreed to see Corvin. But with his increased powers, she figured he could do pretty much whatever he wanted to, whether she let him or not.

"Harrison is back?" Corvin prompted.

"Yeah. Showed up at the cottage. I wasn't expecting him. Freaked me out to have him appear there!"

"I would imagine so. You think you're safe, not that you're going to have to defend yourself against intruders in your own home. It's locked up tight, you have protective wards; you should be allowed to have your own private space. Not to have another race sticking their noses in where they aren't wanted."

"So… how much do you know about them?"

"Them?"

"The immortals. Do you have some other name for them? Can you tell me about their history and… I don't know… explain to me how it all works."

Corvin considered this. He sipped his drink. "Well… lots of rumors and stories, but not so much that is known for certain. There have always been stories about gods, demigods, and other beings with unusual mental, psychic, or spiritual abilities walking the earth. Think of the myths of Buddha, Jesus, and whole pantheons of gods visiting the earth. What are they? Have they always been here? Are they dying out?" He shrugged. "There are more questions than answers."

"That's not at all helpful. You must know something about them… their interactions with humans. Their powers, their rules…"

"I don't think there are a lot of rules, to tell the truth. They seem to do pretty much what they want."

"Harrison said that they weren't allowed to hurt each other."

"But throughout history, we have stories that say that they did. There are a lot of stories of wars, battles, and jealousies between them. There may be rules against it, but I don't think that stops them."

"That's kind of what he said," Reg agreed. "Just like enacting laws doesn't keep people from breaking them. But what about punishments? Are there consequences for breaking the rules? Or can they interfere with humans however they like, and no one cares?"

"Most of the rules are about their interaction with each other, not with humans. I think humans are pretty... inconsequential to them. We are fragile, short-lived creatures. There are too many of us. We're more like cockroaches to them then than cousins."

"Except we don't procreate with cockroaches."

Corvin's brows went up. "No. That's true. There have been punishments and consequences... immortals bound or banished... efforts to curtail their powers by cutting them into pieces so that they can't re-form. But on the whole... the stories make them seem more like petty children than all-powerful beings."

Reg looked away, thinking about that. Corvin's words resonated with her. Harrison was childlike in many ways. And if there were no consequences for them, why would they be any different? They could afford to do whatever they liked.

She watched a couple of women at the bar. They were stunningly beautiful. One was blond, but it seemed like something had reacted with her bleach, because it had a greenish tint to it. When she moved and her skin caught the light, it too seemed slightly green and iridescent. Was she a fairy? Reg had never seen fairies in such a casual setting. They didn't associate with humans in that way, and whatever interactions they had with each other were out of sight. Reg imagined they were stiff and formal even in private, as she had seen them in public.

The other woman was a brunette, with hair in long, loose curls that fell around her face and shoulders. She had a white sheath dress with a neckline that plunged so far Reg could hardly pull her eyes away.

The waiter returned to take their dinner orders. Reg pointed to a picture, answered his questions about how she wanted the fish steaks prepared and what sides she wanted. Corvin placed his order, long and detailed. The waiter collected their menus and left them alone once more. Reg looked back at Corvin, sighing.

"You must know more," she said. "You took the Witch Doctor's powers. So you know a lot more about what they can do. Maybe you got some memories or instincts from him too. What did you learn?"

Corvin tapped his glass with his fingernail, considering. He gave her a warm smile, and Reg felt her attention sliding away as she started to admire his facial features, the warmth around him, the memories of that one night coming back and tempting her to spend another with him. She looked away and carefully built a wall to keep his charms out. She told herself that she couldn't feel them. He was just a man like any other, and she was trying to have a conversation with him. He was distracting her for a reason.

"Quit that and answer my question. I'm not going to forget what I asked."

He looked at her for a moment, waiting for his magic to over-come her, then dropped his gaze.

"There are problems with imbibing so much power," he admitted. "I don't have the same clarity of purpose and ability to control it. Like trying to carry too much at a time, it gets heavy and unwieldy. Or when you have eaten a big meal, and instead of feeling pleasant and satiated, it just hurts, and you want it out again."

"Really." She studied him, reading his face for the truth. Was it just another of his lines, trying to make her feel sorry for him so that he would yield to him? "So you want to give up some of your powers?"

He smiled at her. "You want some?"

On the one hand, it made her curious. Could she take on someone else's powers like he had taken on hers if he offered them to her? She remembered how it had been when he'd fed his own back into her. Could he do that with any of the powers he held? Not just her own?

But she also knew that the moment he put his hands on her or pulled her in for a kiss, she would be in his control. She wouldn't be able to stop him from taking her powers instead of giving her his.

"No. That doesn't sound like a good idea."

He nodded his understanding. "It is hard to sort through what I have and to figure out how to use them and put them to the best use. It's easier in times of emotion. When I was angry and fighting him, that's when instinct took over, and I just did what came naturally."

"Is that what it's like for them? Are they more powerful or capable when they are angry?"

"Perhaps. I'm not sure. History would suggest that they can be very powerful and cruel when in a temper. They can do things that they would come to regret later."

They people-watched in silence, considering the conversation but not speaking. Reg was fascinated by the two women at the bar. All of the men who entered their orbit seemed to be entranced by them. Not just interested in a couple of beautiful faces and bodies, but under a spell, like Corvin held over women.

"Who are they?" Reg asked, noticing that Corvin was watching them as well. He seemed to be far enough away not to be taken in by them, but he was still interested. "Do you know them?"

"I don't know them, no… They don't usually hunt here."

Reg swallowed. "Hunt? Are they… like you, then?"

"No." He shook his head but took no offense at her words. "Not like me. They don't want powers; they want flesh."

"Ick. Really? I assume you're not just talking about… the seafood."

"No. If they try to take anyone from here, the management will stop them, have them ejected. But if they lay in wait outside… they might drag some poor soul away without being caught."

"How can you sit there and let it go on? Shouldn't we do something?"

"Do what?"

"You're the one with powers. Why don't you… tell them to get out of here and not come back. Why don't you magick them into leaving and make it so they are distracted if they ever think of coming here again. You can't just let them…"

"They haven't done anything. It isn't against any law for them to sit in a restaurant. No one can do anything unless they try to drag someone out. And even then… it's hard to do anything but tell them they're breaking the treaty and have to return to the water."

"What are they, then? Some kind of water fairies? What are those water spirits called, naiads?"

"No, they are not naiads, although the naiads would probably act similarly if they were able to go far from their springs and slews."

"What, then?"

"You can't guess?" he challenged.

Reg looked back at them again. She had always enjoyed learning about mythology, but she had a hard time wrapping her mind around the fairy tales and myths becoming real in Black Sands. It was one thing to read a children's story for enjoyment, but quite another to be confronted with monsters and immortals in real life.

"No, just tell me. What are they?"

"The green one is a mermaid. The brunette is a siren."

Reg immediately craned her neck to see the green woman's feet. She was wearing high heeled pumps, a brilliant jade green, but had feet just like any other woman.

"They don't have flippers out of the water," Corvin told her with a grin. "And actually, having them even in water is pretty rare. A recessive gene mutation. Of course, those are the ones sailors could recognize readily, so those are the ones who got all of the attention in literature and art."

"She's a mermaid?"

"You don't think so?"

"Well… I guess so. I just didn't know." She looked at the brunette. "I don't remember much about sirens. They have a powerful song that can distract sailors and make them jump into the ocean."

Corvin nodded. "Yes. Two beautiful races with all the wiles necessary to capture a man."

"But aren't there male mermaids and sirens? Mermen and… I don't know. Guy sirens."

"In some cases, yes; but they are not the hunters. It is the women who… bring home the bacon… so to speak."

"Ugh." Reg grimaced. Was he expecting her to eat? All of the talk about predators and flesh was getting to her. She wasn't sure she'd even be able to look at the fish when the waiter brought it to her. She should have done as she had planned and gone with a salad.

She averted her eyes and shook her head. No more watching the two women. She couldn't bear to watch them tempt some man out of the restaurant and then to try to drag him into the ocean.

When she'd been read fairy tales as a child, she'd always thought how amazing the magical world sounded. So many treasures, magic that turned people beautiful or made them fall in love, talking animals, fairy princesses. Of course, there were also children being lured into the forest to be eaten by a witch or some ferocious beast.

Reg had always told herself that she couldn't be tricked like that. She would always leave a trail back home, and if any old hag tried to hurt her, Reg would punch her straight in the nose and run like hell.

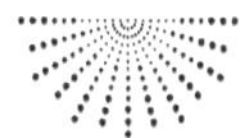

*D*espite her misgivings, Reg's stomach rumbled when the waiter set her dinner plate in front of her. She inhaled the fragrant steam and sighed. "This is the best. I don't think I could ever be vegetarian."

Corvin eyed her. She knew what he was thinking, but he kept the comment to himself. She didn't need him to remind her that she was confirming what he had told her before. That it was in his nature to consume the powers of others just as much as it was in her nature to eat the fish that was on the plate in front of her. Changing that about him would have been trying to change what he was. And no one could change what he was. It was built into his genetic code. If genes were how magical nature was passed from father to son.

They ate in silence for a few minutes, each appreciating their meals. Corvin took a drink.

"So what did you learn from Harrison? Did he tell you anything, or was it all just more questions?"

Reg sighed. "He answered some things. But they were things I didn't want to know. The things that I want to understand, he doesn't answer or says he doesn't know, which is stupid, because he's supposed to be all-knowing and all-powerful, isn't he?"

Corvin cut a neat bite out of his scallops. "I think you're confusing immortals with the Christian god. The Greeks and other cultures with a pantheon of gods never claimed that they were all-knowing or all-powerful. Sometimes they were remarkably short-sighted. They just claimed that they couldn't be killed, or if they could, it was only temporary."

"So Harrison doesn't know everything."

"Obviously not."

"Just like the Witch Doctor didn't know where to find Weston."

Corvin looked up at that. He laid down his fork for a moment. "And who, may I ask, is Weston?"

"You don't know him?"

"How would I know him?"

"I thought if there were stories about all of these immortals, you would already know who he was. There aren't any stories about him?"

"I don't know. They are often known by many different names. They might have different names and different roles in one culture. And then when you add in multiple cultures, there are even more. I would have to know more about his nature and the things he has done. Then I might be able to figure out his other names."

"I don't know much about him. I know that he's… not exactly hiding from the Witch Doctor, but hidden. He broke the rules and so he was bound. Or bound himself. Somehow there was a consequence, and he was hidden from the others."

"Who wanted to do what to him?"

"He and Harrison are friends, I think. But the Witch Doctor is an enemy, and he hoped to destroy Weston while he was still… in hibernation or whatever kind of state he was in. But the Witch Doctor couldn't find him, and Weston didn't manage to get out of this prison he's in. Harrison and the Witch Doctor thought that he would be near Norma Jean so that she could let him out. But he wasn't. Or if he was, they couldn't find him. That's why… the

Witch Doctor killed her. Or why he tortured her, anyway. I think he killed her just because he could."

Corvin nodded, scratching his whiskered chin. "That's all very interesting… so he's been banished or bound… but they expected him to build a back door, or to be able to escape from it by now. Maybe years ago."

Reg nodded.

"And why were you and Harrison talking about Weston? Why didn't you want to know about him? Or was it just unimportant information and you wanted something that affected you."

Reg looked down at her plate and toyed with the next bite of fish, wondering how much she wanted to reveal to Corvin. If he knew enough, he might be willing to help and might have some relevant information. But she didn't like to share anything about her personal life, and particularly about the immortal who now appeared to be her father.

"It seems like his fate is tied up with mine," she hedged.

That wasn't a lie. And if he thought about it, then it was apparent that Weston's existence had affected Reg and the course of her life. Things would have been very different for her if she had grown up with her biological mother.

"And… what? Do you need to find him? Do you have a mission? Harrison thinks that when Weston comes back, it will affect you somehow?"

"I don't know. So… can I change the topic? I don't know much more about Weston, but I had another question."

"Okay… what is it?"

Reg furrowed her brow, thinking about what she wanted and what he might know. "I have questions about cats. Particularly about Starlight."

"I don't know anything about cats."

"Of course you do. You know about everything. At least some things about everything."

He smiled tolerantly. "You think that buttering me up will get me to answer your questions?"

"Of course. You have a big ego. You won't be able to help yourself."

"Wanna bet?"

Reg looked at him, waiting. She didn't look away. Eventually, he broke.

"What exactly do you want to know about cats, and Starlight in particular?"

"You said once that maybe Starlight was a reincarnate. That he had been a human in a previous life."

"I don't remember that. I was probably joking."

"Does that mean that cats *can't* be reincarnated humans?"

"No. Of course he could be."

"How would we be able to tell?"

"Sometimes there are clues in a person's or animal's behavior as to who they were in a previous life. If that soul was very strong."

"I'm pretty sure that Starlight was someone Harrison used to know in a past life."

"It's not out of the realm of possibility. As an immortal, Harrison has likely been around for a very long time."

Reg's brain jumped ahead and she discarded her planned question to address that. "How long have immortals been around? Are there... new immortals and old ones? Where do new ones come from?"

"I don't claim to know much about immortal physiology or reproduction. I imagine they are created in much the same way as humans."

"I don't think so. Harrison was pretty ambiguous about... conception."

Corvin's eyes twinkled. "You brought it up with him?"

"In Greek mythology, the gods weren't all conceived and born like humans, were they? Didn't Athena... spring full-grown from Zeus's head?"

"Yes. And there were also cases of demigods or creatures being born from the sea or other non-human, non-god parents," Corvin admitted.

"So maybe it isn't exactly like with humans. Maybe they can create offspring as they like. Or through various means."

"Maybe."

"So their progeny might not have their DNA. Or their powers."

"I thought we were talking about cats."

"We—oh yeah. I got sidetracked." Reg shook her head. If she pursued the subject of children of the immortals, Corvin was bound to start wondering why. "So… cats as reincarnated humans. Do you think Starlight really could have been a human in a previous life?"

"Sure he could. But why does it matter? In this life, he's a cat."

"Harrison said that he was a very ancient, wise soul."

"Great. So you have a very ancient, wise soul in the body of a cat. He still acts like a cat. He still is a cat. What has changed?"

"Well… I don't know. Do you think *he* could be Weston?"

"Immortals don't die, let alone get reincarnated as cats."

"But if the Witch Doctor could be turned into nine kittens, then why couldn't Weston be a cat too?"

"Well, that's not precisely what happened. The Witch Doctor's power and presence was sent into the draugr kattakyns, and so—"

"So now he's nine kittens," Reg said flatly.

"Well, okay. Now he's nine kittens."

"So why couldn't Weston be one cat? Maybe someone turned him into a cat. Maybe he turned himself into a cat or put his soul into a cat."

"What makes you think that Weston is Starlight?"

"Well… the way that he responded to me at the animal shelter, when he didn't respond to anyone else. He picked me out more than I picked him. Maybe that's because I'm his… our fates are intertwined. Maybe he somehow planned this, that I would meet him in his next life as a cat, and then… I don't know. I have no idea what would happen next."

"You would pet him and feed him and change his litter box for him."

Reg wrinkled her nose. "Corvin!"

"He's a cat. Like I said, if he is Weston, then what changes?"

"I don't know. Maybe he… can communicate with me. Tell me about what happened in his past life. Why he did what he did."

"Which was…?"

Reg wasn't about to reveal any of that. "Break the rules. Become bound. And then… I don't know. If I knew, I wouldn't have to ask him."

"Right." Corvin took a few more bites of his meal. "This is quite a metaphysical discussion for the Port of Call."

"Would it be better somewhere else?"

"At your cottage," he said promptly. "You could even involve Starlight in the conversation if you like. You could take him home a piece of fish and tell him that you wouldn't give it to him until he told you all about his previous life."

"How would he tell me?"

"I assume… telepathically. Since he can't hold a pencil or speak."

"But he doesn't communicate telepathically. I mean, he communicates psychically sometimes, but not in words and sentences. Just in… feelings… nudges."

"Then how do you expect him to tell you about his previous life, whether it was as Weston or someone else?"

Reg sighed. "I don't know. It was just an idea."

"Harrison is the one who can answer your questions, not Starlight."

"And he won't. Or he doesn't. He pretends that he does, giving me some vague or impossible answer, and then smiles like he just gave me the wisdom of the ages. It's frustrating."

"Maybe you and I could put our heads together and come up with something. After all, I do have the powers of an immortal. Maybe I can… compel him."

"I don't think they can compel each other to do anything, do you?"

"No," he admitted, "probably not. But it would still be fun to try."

"By putting our heads together, do you mean putting all of my power into your head?"

"Now, there is an entrancing idea."

"No. Forget it. I came out to dinner with you to keep you company, not to give you my powers."

He motioned to the waiter for another drink. "Don't you find it… cumbersome? Don't those powers weigh down on you at times? It is a big responsibility, and using them takes so much energy out of you…"

His words were soothing and persuasive. Reg caught herself thinking about what it would be like to be a normal human without any psychic powers. How nice it would be to have her brain to herself and not have to worry about all of the other voices.

She pushed back against the idea, scowling at Corvin. "I know what it's like to have them taken away, and it didn't feel good. It didn't feel freeing or nice at all. It was horrible."

For a brief moment, his brows pushed down and the corners of his mouth fell as if he too were remembering what it was like to be drained of powers and be left with nothing but hollowness inside. He quickly masked the expression and looked away from Reg. The waiter brought Corvin a refill and he sipped it, looking over at the bar to see how the ladies were faring.

Reg didn't want to look, but felt compelled. She turned her head and saw that there was a sailor or fisherman with them, his movements drunk and sloppy, leaning on the bar and practically crawling into the siren's lap. He was drooling slightly, his eyes wide and gaze fixed.

"Uh-oh," Reg said.

"Looks like they've got one on the hook," Corvin observed. He lifted his chin and caught the eye of the bartender farther down the bar. The bartender nodded that he was aware of the situation. Corvin looked back at Reg.

"I would normally want to linger over coffee. But I think we might want to leave before things get ugly."

They had both made short work of their meals. And he was right; she didn't like to rush out, but she also didn't want to see what happened to the man or to the mermaid and siren. It wasn't going to be pretty.

"Yeah. I think we should."

"We can stop in for coffee or a drink somewhere else."

Reg nodded her agreement. Corvin raised a hand to signal one of the waiters. Things were suddenly very busy, but the waiter came over, eyebrows raised.

"Your bill?" he suggested.

Corvin inclined his head. "Please."

"Everybody wants to clear out of here all of a sudden," the young man observed. He glanced over his shoulder toward the bar, sweat glistening on his forehead.

"Why don't you call the police?" Reg demanded. "Say that they're being disruptive or acting suspiciously."

"I'm just a waiter, ma'am, I'm not in charge here."

"Nothing the police could do," Corvin advised. "They would come here, see a couple of lovely women, and probably kick the sailor out. They wouldn't understand what is going on."

"Why isn't there a magical police force? This is ridiculous. Everybody knows what's happening; why do they act like ostriches, sticking their heads in the sand?"

"You know, I don't think ostriches actually do that."

Reg glowered at him.

The waiter tapped their order into a hand-held credit card terminal and handed it to Corvin. He glanced at it, punched a few buttons and, in a moment, the waiter was handing him a receipt. They got up and made their way toward the door, along with several other couples who were looking pale and anxious.

"There is no magical police force because it would never work," Corvin explained, as they hit the cool night air and walked toward the car. "It's been tried in several different forms.

Humans are the most interested in such things, but you can't have a group of humans administering justice for a dozen different races. It doesn't work. What you end up with isn't just racial prejudice, but war. We have treaties that are supposed to give each race the autonomy they need to follow their cultural norms and physical needs. Allow us to live side-by-side without interfering with each other's rights and freedoms any more than necessary."

"And that includes letting a sailor be dragged out of a restaurant by a mermaid and a siren? To be killed and eaten?"

"No. I told you, they will take action once the ladies reach that point. They'll do their best to see to the safety of that man. But until they attempt to take him, they haven't done anything wrong."

Reg got into the car when he opened the door for her. She sat with her lips pressed tightly shut, not saying all of the things that she wanted to. They needed to overhaul their entire system. How could there not be a way to stop the mermaid and the siren from doing what they were?

"Look," Corvin said after he got in and started the engine. "Even if all of the parties involved were human, what would you suggest doing? The police can't arrest someone they think is a serial killer without some evidence. They can't just take a call from a little old lady who thinks that her neighbor is up to no good and go out and arrest him. They can investigate, but they need evidence of wrongdoing before they can take any action. You can't arrest someone because you think they looked at a child the wrong way. You need to wait until he takes some action to kidnap or harm the child. You can't arrest someone you think is going to drink too much and get into their car until they actually get behind the wheel. We can't do anything about the mermaid and the siren until they do something that crosses the boundaries. And those boundaries have become very strictly defined over the past centuries."

"People take matters into their own hands all the time. Vigilantes. Cops who think they know better. Why isn't there anyone in there who dares to do what is right?"

"They are doing what is right. None of us like it, but you can't do anything about what people are thinking. You can't just start killing every mermaid who shows up in a bar, or go out hunting and killing every mermaid within a hundred-mile radius to ensure that they don't encroach on the land. Those things have been done in the past, and it doesn't make us safer. It just increases the violence between our societies. More people will get killed in a war with the mermaids than are killed by their hunting."

"That's ridiculous."

"I didn't see you walking up to them and challenging them to a battle."

"I don't mean that. I mean… telling them to leave. You can tell someone to move on. Homeless people get kicked out of stores and restaurants all the time. Owners have the right to refuse them service."

"And do you think that a mermaid is just going to agree to leave? They are a bloody race, Reg. A bloody, violent race. Don't get caught up by all of the Disney sweetness. They make movies about cuddly lions and bears, too. Does that make them good pets for your children?"

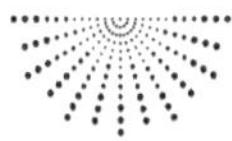

CHAPTER SEVENTEEN

Reg brooded silently as they drove to a small coffee house and sat down. When she had her coffee in front of her, Reg couldn't hold it inside any longer.

"You know what? I hate this place. I regret that I ever came here. I thought that I was coming to a nice little town with a higher-than-normal population of confidence scams relating to magic. I didn't expect to find… real magic, predatory magical races, and dangers out of a fairy tale. I just wanted to live a nice quiet life and be able to make a good living for once."

"And instead, you find pixies and draugar and mermaids," Corvin finished.

"Exactly. All of these things, when you read about them in children's books, they are so much fun. You think that living in a fairy world would be… magical—beautiful happily-ever-after endings for everyone. But fairies aren't cute little sparkly creatures flying around your head and granting wishes. They're…"

"Haughty and self-absorbed and rarely care to have any inter-action with humans."

"Yeah." Reg thought about Lord Bernier and knew that she was being unfair. He hadn't had to step in to save her from Corvin or to appear at his hearing to testify against him. That had been his choice, and even if he did think of her as a child, he had done what was right when nobody had asked him to. And she remembered how the pixie Karol Blackmoor had been so intent on getting her sister back, on reversing the spell that had turned Calliopia into a fairy so that she could return to her pixie family. The other races had good qualities too, even if they were not kindly disposed toward humans. "I don't know what to think. It's so different from what I expected. And from what I would have expected if I had known that there was real magic and real fairies and everything. I want it to be normal, or to be... non-violent, with everyone living together harmoniously."

"Have you ever been in a family where everyone got along together without any arguing or fighting?" Corvin challenged.

Reg laughed. "No! Not even close."

"And they were all human—or at least, I assume they were. If humans cannot even get along with each other without conflict, how do you expect humans and other races to live together without running into some problems?"

"I don't know. Disney again, I guess. In the movies, you have good and bad, but the dividing lines are obvious. The humans are always going to be on the side of good, except for one or two bad apples. And the fairies are good. You might have trolls or mischievous elves, but they can always be defeated by the good guys in a single battle. You know who the bad guys are because they wear black and are accompanied by ominous music and evil laughter."

"Well, that would all make real life pretty interesting. But in real life, you don't have one race that is good and one that is bad. They each have their good points and bad. Things that conflict with each other's societies. You have to make compromises and rules if you are going to live side-by-side as peacefully as possible."

Reg nodded. She was beginning to see that he was right. They had developed their interspecies laws and treaties over many years, coming to the best compromises and set of rules that they could.

But she didn't have to like it.

"And the bad guys aren't always wearing black," Corvin pointed out with a smile.

Reg was reminded that he was dressed all in black, as he usually was.

At least Disney got that part right.

She took a long sip of her coffee. She probably shouldn't be drinking coffee so late in the day, but she was becoming resigned to the fact that she wouldn't get to sleep until two or three in the morning anyway, so there was no need to curtail her caffeine intake just because it was early evening.

"And then there are immortals," she said bitterly, "who apparently don't need to follow any rules about interacting with humans, other than not having babies with them."

Corvin's brows went up.

The bells over the coffee shop jangled and Reg let herself be distracted, glancing over to see who had come in. Someone safe or another magical race that was going to cause conflict? A human sitting down to visit with family or friends or to read a book? Or a troll intent on raising havoc?

Or worse yet… it was Damon.

* * *

Damon saw Reg a moment after she saw him. He wasn't pleased. Reg felt herself flush. How many times had she told him that she didn't want anything to do with Corvin and she wasn't going to get involved with him? And yet, there she was, sitting with him in an intimate little after-dinner conversation. As if they were best friends and she didn't have a care in the world. As if he couldn't consume her powers, leaving her an empty husk.

Corvin took in Reg's reaction and turned in his seat to see who had just come in. His mouth tightened and, for a moment, she was sure that he was going to accuse her of inviting Damon to join her.

Damon was by himself. He hesitated for a moment, looking at

Reg and Corvin, then went up to the counter to place his order. Reg looked for something to say to Corvin to hide the fact that they were both waiting to see what Damon was going to do. She couldn't manage to pick up the thread of the conversation again. After Damon got his large cup of coffee, he walked over to their table.

"Reg, good to see you. I didn't know you were going to be here."

"Uh… neither did I. We just…" She didn't want to describe the scene at the Port of Call or to tell him that she and Corvin had not just gone out for coffee, but for dinner too.

"Just coincidence," Corvin said smoothly. "We hadn't particularly made plans to be here."

"You just met up by accident, then? Ran into each other?"

He was looking at Reg, not Corvin. Reg didn't answer. If she lied, he would know it.

"How about you?" Corvin asked. "Just out to top off the gas? Not meeting anyone?"

Reg felt the subtle jab. Corvin was there with Reg, who Damon had been dating, and Damon was there all alone.

"I was guarding at the Conjurecraft Conference all day. Surprised I didn't see you there." Damon allowed a couple of beats to pass. "Oh, right. You don't currently hold membership in any coven."

Ouch. Reg could see Corvin grinding his teeth and could feel the anger rising off of him. Damon shouldn't be provoking him like that, but Corvin *had* started it. The trouble was, if Corvin blew, who knew what kind of harm he could do to Damon. He had already observed that his magic was easier to manage when he was angry.

Reg looked from one to the other anxiously. Had she escaped the violence at the Port of Call only to have to witness a war between the two warlocks? She cleared her throat and addressed them in a voice that pretended to be much more confident than it was.

"Put the wands away, boys. I can talk to who I want to. I don't belong to either one of you."

Neither of them was willing to back down first. Reg raised her eyebrows and gave them both a stern look. She wished that she could manage 'the look' that foster moms had always given her. That one that would make even the most stubborn and recalcitrant teen back down and drop his eyes.

It was Damon who broke first. He looked away from Reg.

"I know I don't own you," he agreed. "It isn't that. I'm just concerned about you. We both know how dangerous Hunter can be…"

"It's my choice who I associate with and whether I ask for your help or not. And I didn't."

"I don't get it. You're willing to become his thrall? You give up?"

"I haven't given up. But I'm tired of running away. I don't like running."

Damon eyed Corvin, who sat back with a smirk that indicated he had won the contest and Reg had chosen him.

"You think you're so slick?" Damon demanded. He threw a card down on the table in front of Corvin. "She's seeing Davyn Smithy too. Did you know that?"

Corvin's eyes dropped to the business card and he frowned. He looked back at Reg. She was not about to explain to him why she had met with Davyn. Just thinking about the meeting made her feel sick, especially when she remembered how hard she had pushed back, insisting that they needed to do something to protect people from Corvin, and there she was sitting across from him as if her words had meant nothing at all.

Corvin and Damon obviously interpreted her guilty look to mean something else. Both of them were now angry not just at each other, but at her.

"Look," she said, "I can meet with who I want about what I want. It's none of your business. I don't have a relationship with

Davyn Smithy. I could, if I wanted to, though, and neither of you would have any say in it."

Neither of them had to like it either. Clearly, they didn't. That was fine with Reg. If they were both going to be so jealous and act like teenage boys, then maybe she needed to find someone who was more mature and able to have a trusting relationship with her. She shook her head.

"I'm going to get a cab home. This is ridiculous."

"So you didn't just run into each other here," Damon said triumphantly.

"I didn't say we did. Back off, Damon. If you're going to keep showing up and accusing me of having relationships with other people, then I've had it. Enough is enough. I'm done with you. I'm done with both of you."

She stood up. Luckily, her path was unimpeded; she didn't need Corvin or Damon to move out of the way for her. She walked away from them, feeling grimly satisfied with herself. She didn't have to choose between them. She didn't have to date either one of them. If they thought that fighting over her was going to get her worked up, they were wrong. The rivalry didn't excite her.

She assumed that once she had walked away from them, there would be no point in their continuing the conversation. Damon would pick up his coffee and walk out. Corvin would finish his or leave it on the table, and with a shrug, get back into his big black car and go home. Or maybe back to the Port of Call to see how things had ended up there.

There was a long moment of silence, as she assumed they both watched her walk away and decided that pursuit wasn't going to bring her back. But then Corvin let out an incoherent shout of anger, and Reg whirled around to protect herself from attack.

Corvin swept the little table out of his way so that there was only empty space between him and Damon. Damon was looking at him, but not defending himself, not acting like there was any danger in his standing there.

Whatever Corvin was seeing enraged him. He clawed at the

air in front of him, making grunts of protest and tried to shove something invisible out of the way. Reg blinked. Damon was feeding a vision into Corvin's head, but Reg didn't know what it was. She couldn't see it herself, even when she strained for a glimpse. Damon kept her blocked out.

Corvin fought more frantically. Damon grinned, thoroughly enjoying himself as he watched Corvin fight the empty air in front of him. Reg tried to signal to him to stop. Nothing good could come of enraging Corvin. Especially not with the increase in his powers.

Then Corvin apparently broke through the vision, and he knew exactly what had happened and where the images had come from. He launched himself at Damon and, even though Reg was several steps away, she flinched and backed away as far as she could. There were a few other customers in the shop watching with wide-eyed interest. The baristas ducked behind the counter and then peeked over it to keep an eye on the action. Reg didn't know if anyone was calling the police yet, but it wouldn't be long before the thought occurred to someone.

But she was more concerned about what damage Corvin could do to Damon than anything else. She watched them anxiously. If it was just a physical fight, she didn't need to worry. But if Corvin unleashed his magic on his opponent, there could be dire consequences.

"Corvin. Corvin!"

She had to yell to make herself heard over their scuffling, growls, and curses. Corvin looked across the room at Reg, scowling. Like he couldn't understand what she would be objecting to.

"Just stop," Reg urged. "Come on; this is stupid."

"He is an untrained young pup who ought to learn to have some respect for his elders!" Corvin snapped.

Damon laughed. "I should have respect for you? For someone who has no powers of his own and only steals them from others? You are the lowest kind of witch. A bottom feeder."

Corvin swept his hand toward Damon, and Reg saw in a fraction of an instant that he wasn't just waving him away. She could see the energy gather around Corvin's hand, and she was immediately there, holding him back. But not physically. She hadn't actually moved from her spot. She stopped him without moving a muscle.

Corvin looked across the room at her again, furious at her holding him back. She could feel him struggling to break free of her psychic hold, going rapidly through his new powers and gifts to find one that would combat her hold on him. It wouldn't be long before he succeeded.

Damon had ducked, also sensing the magical energy that Corvin had been about to throw in his direction. The Witch Doctor had nearly killed Damon. Maybe Corvin would have gotten the job done.

When Damon realized that something had stopped Corvin and was holding him back, he looked around, eyes wide. He realized that it was Reg's doing and laughed again.

"Looks like you've got your hands full with this one," he mocked Corvin. "She's no damsel in distress. Good luck with that!"

"Just get out of here, Damon," Reg urged. "I don't know how long I can do this."

Damon took his time getting to the door. He looked back one last time before exiting, smirking at Corvin. Then he was gone.

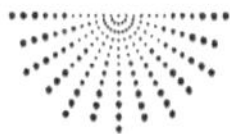

When Damon was gone, Reg looked at Corvin uncertainly. She wasn't sure what would happen when she released him from her hold. Her upbringing had trained her to run when there was trouble, and she prepared to do that. But before she could let go of him, she felt Corvin's effort slacken, and he stopped fighting her. Reg released her hold and watched him warily, measuring the distance to the door. Unfortunately, he had a car and she didn't. But she could get through narrow alleys and jump fences. There were ways to lose a car if she had enough lead time.

"What a little weasel," Corvin said, shaking his head.

Reg still didn't move. Around them, people were starting to talk again, still watching covertly. The baristas were popping up behind the counter.

"We should probably go," Reg suggested.

"Shall we try for restaurant number three?"

"Please, no."

Corvin chuckled. He lifted the table he had knocked down and put it back in place. He arranged the chairs around it. There was coffee all over the floor from their spilled drinks, but Reg's and Corvin's mugs had not broken. They probably saw a lot of rough handling throughout the day and they were very sturdy. Corvin went up to the counter and pulled several bills out of his wallet, handing them to the nearest employee.

"Sorry about that. And the mess."

The employee took the money, nodding wordlessly. Corvin touched Reg lightly on the back, sending an electrical shock straight up her spine, and they walked out to his car. He silently opened and held her door for her and then got into the driver's seat.

"Well," he said eventually, when they had almost reached Reg's house. "That was an eventful evening."

"It was. I guess... I learned a lot." She closed her eyes, thinking about Damon, who she was sure would not be knocking on her door again. And Corvin, who would now expect to be invited into the cottage, but she couldn't take that risk. She'd done enough risky things for one evening and, while she had been able to hold Corvin back, she wasn't sure how much longer her power would last. Then she wouldn't be able to prevent him from charming her. "What a night."

"I'm sorry it ended on such a sour note." Corvin looked over at Reg, his expression sheepish. "I don't generally... act that way. I know I have a temper, but I usually control it better."

"You probably don't usually have someone feeding images directly into your brain, either. What exactly did he show you?"

"Despite what he did, I should still have kept it under control. What is he? Just an untrained young pup trying out his powers and showing off for a girl. I've been around longer than his parents. You would think that my experience would give me some control."

She had seen him so angry before. But not violent. When he fought the Witch Doctor, he had been powerful and focused, but not out of control. Reg held her hands together in her lap to stop them from vibrating. The whole thing had shaken her up far more than she would like to admit. She wanted to think that she was tough and unflappable, that she could deal with anything. But a physical threat still sent her into a tailspin, flashing back to the violence she had seen or experienced as a child.

* * *

Corvin pulled in front of Sarah's house. He looked at her. "Are you all right?"

"I'll be fine. Watch an old movie before bed to relax. Have some tea." Or some whiskey. That might help her to sleep better.

"I know that we're not… an item, Regina… but I can't help feeling possessive. Not just because you're attractive and I like you, but also because of your gifts. I can't help feeling like they should be mine. They were mine, once."

"You held them for a little while, but they were not yours. You took them away from me. You didn't own them and you still don't."

"I paid for them. I compensated you."

"We had a nice evening. That's all. That doesn't mean I owe you anything, especially my powers. So get over it."

He frowned deeply, but he didn't try to argue the point. Maybe he was starting to come around.

Or maybe he was just tired from the fight.

"Can I walk you to your door?"

Reg took a deep breath and let it out. "No magic and you're not coming inside."

"Deal."

She looked over at him, frowning, wondering whether she could trust anything he said. Not that she'd ever been able to. Eventually, she nodded. "Okay. You control yourself."

He didn't touch her as he escorted her down the sidewalk to the cottage, maybe sensing that she would object.

At the door, he hovered close, looking down at her, and she felt his warmth. That feeling of contentment and attraction that she felt whenever he walked into a room. She'd been able to ignore it most of the rest of the night, especially when violence had been threatened, but now that they were at her door, and it was dark, and she was coming down from the adrenaline rush, she was especially vulnerable.

"You should go home now," she told him.

"I will. You sure you'll be okay tonight?"

"You're not coming in."

"I'm sorry for the way things ended up. I shouldn't have lost my temper so badly."

"Yeah. It would have been nice if the two of you could have behaved like mature adults instead of children."

She hadn't seen him move any closer, yet she was sure he had. She could feel his breath on her and the cloying scent of roses was coming off his skin. "No. You said you wouldn't use any magic."

"I can't help my body's autonomic responses. I'm not doing anything to you."

"You can control it. You've said so before."

"Not everything. Some things… a man can't help feeling…"

She pushed him back mentally. It was an effort, after the eventful evening. She tried to build a psychic wall around herself. She could barely find the strength. She tried harder, remembering the feeling of Harrison's protective spell around her. Corvin pushed closer, almost pinning Reg to the door. She fumbled for the doorknob.

"Back off, Corvin. Give me some air."

"Regina…"

She gave one final mental shove. He stepped back, but in a moment had recovered his balance and was back. He took the key from her and tried to fit it into the lock, then looked at it, holding it up in front of his face, frowning.

"What key is this? Where is your house key?" He handed it back.

Reg patted at her pockets, then shoved her hand into her purse and stirred it around, feeling for the ring of keys and listening for the tell-tale clink, keeping her eyes on him. Corvin pulled the purse from her and looked inside.

"What a rat's nest. Here they are." He fished the keys out and fit the house key to the doorknob lock. He pushed it open behind her. Reg stumbled in. It was a relief to get far enough away from him that his breath wasn't right in her face. She felt behind her, moving like she was blind and had never seen the room before. She needed to get in far enough to close the door and then she could relax.

Corvin stepped through the doorway.

Reg gasped in shock. She took another step back. "I didn't invite you in!"

He just smiled.

Reg swore, looking around, trying to figure out a way to defend herself. She didn't carry a weapon or keep one in the cottage. She didn't even have a pocketknife or broken bottle. But she did have a kitchen! Reg moved toward it, keeping her eyes on Corvin, keeping plenty of space between them. The room was already filling with the floral scent, getting more and more stifling. Reg fought back against her natural reaction, telling herself that it was a skunk. It was unpleasant. She didn't want to smell it, and it didn't make her feel good.

She wasn't attracted to Corvin; she didn't have to surrender to him.

"Calm down, Regina," he said softly. "I'm not going to hurt you. Forget about all of that. You and I can be friends. We can sit down and have a chat. I want to make sure that you're all right. You're very pale. It wouldn't be responsible for me to leave you here by yourself without making sure you are okay."

Reg's feet touched the tile of the kitchen. She was close. She darted a glance to the side to measure the distance to the knife drawer, the angle of access, planning in her head how she would move and which knife she would pull.

As much as she abhorred the violence of the evening, she would do whatever she had to to protect herself. She wasn't going to give way to him this time. She was stronger. She had her replica of Harrison's protection spell.

Harrison!

Reg thought of him there in the living room, sitting on the couch, his long legs out, Starlight in his lap. He had been there not twenty-four hours before. She should have asked him for his help in more practical matters. How to protect herself. How to cast simple spells. Instead of having metaphysical discussions about immortals.

"I think it's time for you to leave."

Corvin whirled around and looked at Harrison sitting on the couch, his long legs stretched out in front of him. He had on his striped shirt this time, looking like a mime, an escaped prisoner, or the juggler at a circus. He smiled at Corvin and twisted the ends of his large mustache.

"What are you doing here?" Corvin demanded. "No one was here; we were alone." Frustration had entered his voice. Reg couldn't help smiling at Corvin's tone of betrayal.

"Reg wanted me," Harrison said with a shrug. "Something about a protective spell?"

"Yes," Reg agreed. "I needed your help. I don't know how to cast a spell. I'm not magical, just psychic."

"Pish. You have powers. It doesn't matter what you call them."

They both looked at Corvin.

"It's time for you to go," Reg told him. "You don't need to worry about taking care of me. I have someone here to keep me company now."

Corvin's face contorted with anger. He looked back and forth between them, looking for some way to still get what he wanted. He had been so close; having his prize snatched away right under his nose sent him into a paroxysm of fury.

"Why don't you tell *him* to go?" he demanded, pointing at Harrison. "He is the one who used magic to get in here, who bypassed all of your wards and intruded on your privacy. He should be the one you are kicking out, not me."

"I needed him because you wouldn't listen to me. If you'd behaved yourself like you promised, I wouldn't have needed him."

His hands clenched into fists and he shook his head.

"This is unbelievable! I gave you a nice evening. I protected you from having to see what went down at the Port of Call. I defended your honor. And this is how you repay me? By treating me like a criminal? Implying that I did something wrong? I haven't done anything to harm you."

"You would still take my powers if you had half a chance. Admit it; you can't even think about anything else right now. You want it so badly you can taste it."

"Have I attacked you? You can't accuse me of doing anything just because you can sense my emotions. A person can feel one way and still make a decision the other way."

"Maybe so. But tonight you don't have to be tempted anymore. We're both tired. Maybe that's made your willpower weaken. Just go home."

He rubbed his face and chin. He did look fatigued. Maybe with everything that had happened, his hunger had gotten the better of him when it wouldn't have otherwise. He hesitated, turning partway toward the door.

"This doesn't mean anything. If coming in here to check on you was a mistake, it's just one small mistake. I didn't do anything to you. You know that. You don't know what would have happened next."

"I'm not going to make any decisions about you tonight," Reg said. "Just let me sleep on it."

Until the appearance of Damon, they had been having an enjoyable night. Corvin had behaved himself reasonably well and Reg had been able to resist him until she had gotten too tired. Maybe they could be friends, as long as neither of them got too tired or let their guard down. Corvin started to walk toward the door. Starlight darted out from under one of the wicker chairs and nipped at his calves. Corvin let out a shout and whirled around, trying to swipe at the cat or to kick him.

"That cat! If he's going to attack me like that, he's going to get hurt!"

"Poor Corvin," Reg said in fake sympathy. "Being attacked by the nasty kitty! If you do anything to hurt Starlight, you can forget about us ever being friends. I mean it. I will never talk to you again."

Corvin glared at Starlight, who had taken refuge behind the kitchen island. Starlight peered around the corner, the emotions emanating from him just as strong as the ones coming from Corvin. He was definitely not having warm fuzzy thoughts about the warlock.

Corvin scowled. He turned and stalked out without another word, slamming the door behind him.

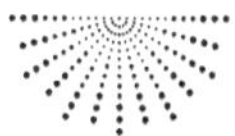

*R*eg looked at Harrison. "Thank you for coming."

"I didn't have anything better to do."

"Well… good. I don't mean to call on you whenever something bad happens, but I didn't know what else to do."

"You were upset after we talked."

"Yeah, I was."

"That's why you went with the spirit-eater?" He shook his head slowly. "I will never understand human emotions."

"I'm not sure I can explain it myself. I wanted to… prove that I could take care of myself and that I could make my own decisions. It wasn't all just… fate and immortals."

"You made your own choice."

"I knew it wasn't a smart one at the time. But I didn't care."

"Are all humans as confusing as you?"

"Maybe not. I'm kind of… nonconforming."

He nodded. He made a sort of a purring sound and Starlight came running from behind the counter and jumped into his lap. Harrison petted him.

"You need to learn to protect yourself against the warlock if you are going to allow him in your home."

"I didn't invite him in. I don't know how he was able to get past the wards. He hasn't been able to before. Do you think he's that much stronger now?"

Harrison raised an eyebrow. "He is much stronger. But he does not yet have control of his powers. Much like you."

Reg shook off the criticism. "Then how did he get past all of the wards?"

He looked slowly around the room. "He did not break them. Therefore, you let him in."

"Those can't be the only two ways for him to get in, because I didn't let him in. I didn't invite him. I didn't allow him. He just… followed me in."

"Maybe you do not remember properly," Harrison suggested kindly.

"It just happened five minutes ago! I haven't forgotten!"

"Humans have very faulty memories. Maybe you were drinking tonight? Or something else happened that might have altered your memories?"

"No! I had a couple of drinks, but not enough to cause any problems with my memory! I know exactly what happened."

He scratched Starlight's ears and bent down to whisper something to the cat. He looked back at Reg. "Tell me what happened, then."

Reg started her narration with when they were still in the car when she had explicitly told Corvin that he would not be coming into the house. Harrison did not seem to find this significant. Reg went on and described his helping her to unlock the door when she had been so shaky.

Harrison nodded. "You see?"

"What?"

"You gave him your key, and he unlocked and opened the door."

"Well… not exactly, but…"

"When you give someone a key, you are giving them permission to enter."

"But… I told him he couldn't come in. I told him I didn't

want him in. Doesn't that mean that I didn't invite him in? Yes, he helped me to find my keys and get the door open, but that doesn't mean that I gave him permission to come into my house."

Harrison steepled his hands together, looking at her. Obviously, that was precisely what it did mean.

"No," Reg protested.

"I am not in charge of human magic," Harrison said. "I did not set the wards or set the conditions of their operation. Your witch friend did that. The wards will only function against those who you do not permit to enter. You permitted the warlock to enter by giving him your keys."

"He took them out of my bag. I didn't exactly give them to him."

"He opened the door with your key. That makes him an invited guest."

"And what if… someone stole my purse and used my key to let themselves into the house. The wards would not work?"

"No. They would not."

Reg stared at him in disbelief.

"A key has potent magic," Harrison explained. "You must always guard your keys well. Anyone who can use it has your authority."

"But… what kind of magic is that? That's stupid!"

"It is ancient magic. For as long as there have been powers, there have been keys."

Reg's head hurt. Maybe she'd had more to drink than she thought. Or maybe it was just everything that had happened. She was tired and confused. Holding off Corvin during the evening and the final struggle against him had been exhausting.

"Fine. Then I guess I invited him in. The invitation doesn't stand, though, does it? Now that he's gone, and he doesn't have my keys, he can't get back in?"

"Correct."

"Okay. Why does it all have to be so complicated? And why can't anyone tell me the rules to start with, instead of everything being a secret and having to figure it all out on my own through trial and error?"

"It is not complicated. It is very simple. You lack knowledge."

Reg growled at that. "I'm going to bed. You do not need to come and tuck me in. And Starlight has been fed, no matter what he might tell you."

Harrison looked at Starlight's face, and Reg knew that he was going to feed Starlight despite her words. Reg put her hand on the counter to steady herself. She looked at the doorway to her bedroom, then back at Harrison.

"Do you have anything else to tell me? If you do, you'd better do it now."

"Have a good sleep, Regina."

She rubbed her eyes. "In the morning, will you show me how to do a proper protection spell against Corvin?"

"If I am here."

"Will you be?"

"We will know when it is tomorrow."

* * *

Reg tossed and turned restlessly. At first, she thought it was because Harrison was there, but later Starlight came in to watch out the window and afterward snuggled with her, so she knew that Harrison must be gone. He definitely preferred Harrison when he was there. Unless Harrison had sent Starlight to watch over Reg as she slept, he must have gone home—or wherever it was that immortals went. Mount Olympus? Hades? She wondered what kind of a place Harrison lived in.

When he disappeared, was he anywhere? Or everywhere? She suspected that he would tell her that she was again conflating the immortals with the Christian god. The immortals were not everywhere. But could they be? Were they somewhere, or were they nowhere or scattered across the universe?

She rolled over, scratched Starlight's ears, and closed her eyes, trying to find that sweet spot so she could find sleep. She had gone to bed too early. She'd been keeping later nights recently, and getting up in the morning was becoming difficult.

"Just go to sleep," she muttered to herself. "You're tired. You want to have the strength to do things tomorrow, especially if Harrison will show you how to do a protection spell. You need to get some rest."

It didn't work. But then, it never did, so she wasn't exactly expecting it to.

Eventually, her brain started to wander from one thing to another, and she knew she was close to sleep. It made illogical leaps and switched from one line of thought to another, and she strove just to let it wander so that eventually she could find the way to dreamland.

And then she was dreaming, and she wasn't happy about it.

"Wake up!" a voice told her, and even though she tried to open her eyes and to look around, it was like her lids were stuck together with superglue. She ignored it and decided to stay asleep.

"Reg, it's not safe. You need to listen to me. Regina!" The voice reached a screech, and Reg found herself pulling away in fear, knowing that physical punishment would follow continued disobedience. But how was she supposed to get the sleep she needed if she let the dream wake her up?

"Are you listening?" The voice was definitely Norma Jean's. "The door. You need to make sure it is locked."

"The door is locked," Reg mumbled, her words thick.

She had locked it after Corvin had gone, hadn't she? It wasn't like he was going to be coming back there anyway. He would go away and sulk and try to come up with another tactic to get what he wanted.

She was safe.

Besides, Harrison was there. He wasn't going to let anyone hurt her. He was her guardian.

"You cannot trust them," Norma Jean's screechy voice lowered to a whisper. "You can't trust any of them. They don't tell the truth."

"Men?"

"Men, angels, immortals, they are all the same. You cannot know what is in their minds. Their lips are lies. All lies."

"When you got pregnant, did you know that Weston was your baby's father? Did you know that he was magical? An immortal?"

"Who knows what they really are? They come in cover of darkness, and they do not let you know who they are behind the mask. All men are like this."

Reg groaned. "Oh, just let me go to sleep, mother. I'm not getting tangled up with any men, so you don't need to worry about that."

"Check the lock. Make sure the door is locked."

Eventually, Norma Jean's shrieks and threats woke Reg up completely. She lay there in bed, waiting for sleep to come back, but the dream kept returning to her and she knew she couldn't get back to sleep until she got up and checked the door.

"The lock, the lock, the lock…" echoed in her head, repeated over and over again in a litany.

Starlight looked up and made a little noise as Reg got out of bed. Hardly able to keep her eyes open, Reg stumbled across the cottage to the front door. Harrison had, she noted, thought to turn off the lights before he had disappeared to wherever it was he went. She got to the door and checked the locks. Both the handle and the deadbolt were in the locked position.

Reg shook her head.

"Crazy ghost. You'd better let me go to sleep now."

* * *

In the morning, she eventually wiped the vestiges of her restless dreams away and got out of bed. Starlight wasn't in the room any longer, and she hoped that might mean that Harrison was on hand and she could get some lessons from him on protecting herself. She had not done too poorly in constructing protective spells since he had first protected her from the Witch Doctor, imitating his spell the best she could, but she didn't know how to make it stronger and wasn't sure she was going about it the right way at all.

When she walked out to the kitchen and looked around, it was apparent that he had not returned. Starlight was standing by the fridge and looked up at her imperiously.

"Well, good morning to you too, your highness. Thank you for letting me sleep in."

He stretched his muscles without changing position, making a little shiver run through him from ears to tail. He waited, drilling into her with his eyes.

"If no one else can tell me who you are or where you came from, maybe you can. Are you Weston?"

He blinked. She didn't get the feeling that he was. He was a cat, and it was silly of her to think that he could be an immortal, especially not the immortal who was her father or had created her.

"No? Were you owned by an immortal? How does Harrison know you?"

No response. Maybe Starlight didn't want to communicate before breakfast. It wasn't like she couldn't figure out what he wanted as he sat by the fridge door waiting for her. Maybe after breakfast, he would find a way to communicate more to her about his past. She had been able to get information from him before, just little bits of ideas, like his name. He was the one who had chosen Starlight, not she. She would probably have ended up naming him something lame like "Tux" or "Whiskers."

Reg added some dry kibble to his bowl, and while he had been eating the pricey brand that she had started to buy, he didn't show any interest in it when she was there to get him something better out of the fridge.

"No spicy chicken today," Reg told him. She opened the fridge, having to push him out of the way with her foot to avoid hitting him. It wasn't like he didn't know where he needed to sit for her to open the fridge unimpeded. He seemed to block it deliberately.

Reg looked inside. There was half a pizza, and she had no idea where it had come from. Harrison didn't drink coffee; did he eat pizza? Did immortals need to eat food? Or could they eat it for enjoyment? She remembered something about a special drink on Mount Olympus. And they had definitely had parties with lots of wine and food. Maybe they could eat if they chose but didn't need to. Maybe Harrison didn't like coffee, but had the same need for physical nourishment as she did. She opened the lid of the pizza.

Meat lover's. Definitely not the gnome, then.

Would immortals be vegetarian? She decided not. If they didn't care what happened to humans and didn't have any rules against hurting them, then she doubted they would have any regulations about hurting non-human animals either. Was it Artemis who was the goddess of the hunt and had led the gods to kill some special kind of deer? Reg shook her head. She pulled out a couple of pieces of pizza for her breakfast and looked in the various bowls in the fridge for something for Starlight's. Spicy Italian sausage would not be a good choice for Starlight, and she had heard that they didn't digest cow's milk very well. That probably applied to cheese as well. She found some roast beef that Sarah had left on Sunday and turned around to put it on the cutting board.

She just about fainted with the shock of seeing Harrison on the other side of the island, helping himself to her pizza.

That answered the question of whether immortals could eat, then.

"Can't you warn me before you appear like that?" she demanded.

"How could I tell you I am here before I am here?" Harrison took a big bite out of the slice of pizza. Reg put a couple more slices on a plate and then into the microwave. She cut up the roast beef for Starlight while she waited for the pizza to warm. When she took it out of the microwave, she could see Harrison's nostrils quivering.

"Do you want yours warmed up too?"

He nodded and pushed his slices toward her. Reg obliged.

"Did you come back to help me with my protection spell?"

"Perhaps."

"I really could use some instruction. I can do a little bit… but I don't know if I'm doing it right."

"If you are able to stop the spirit-eater, you are doing it right."

"Well, that's good. Then I just need to learn how to strengthen it. Or do it when I'm tired."

She waited for the microwave, not wanting to start eating before Harrison had his pizza back. When it beeped, she pulled the plate out and handed it to him. "Now be careful. That will be hot. Don't burn yourself."

Harrison nodded at this wise advice and stood there, staring down at the food.

"We could sit down," Reg offered awkwardly. She rarely sat down at the table to eat, usually standing at the island or sitting down in the living room. But she could act like a civilized person and eat at the table.

But they never got that far.

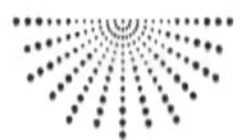

eg's phone started to ring. She looked down at it.

"Oh, it's Francesca. You remember, the charmer, who helped with the draugrs."

Harrison nodded. "I remember her," he agreed. He stared at her phone. "You'd better answer it."

Reg was going to put it off and call Francesca later, but she was struck by the urgency in Harrison's tone. She swiped the phone and answered the call.

"Hi, Francesca."

"Reg? They are gone again! I do not know how they can disappear like this. I know that Nicole doesn't want me to give the kittens away, but that's what we have to do. You and I understand that, why can't she?"

"Maybe because she's a cat. All she has are instincts that tell her to mother the kittens. She probably can't figure out why you would want to take them away."

"If she is smart enough to understand that I want to take them away, she ought to be smart enough to figure out why."

"I think you're just upset. Why don't I come over after we have breakfast, and then—"

Reg didn't even get a chance to finish her sentence. She was still talking into her phone when she was suddenly in Francesca's living room, face-to-face with her. Reg blinked and looked around, not sure what had just happened.

Harrison was a couple of feet away from her and Starlight was there to, bent over like he was still eating from his dish. He put his ears back and looked around.

"What?" Reg shook her head at Harrison. "Did you do that? You can't just transport people across space without warning them!"

Harrison twirled the ends of his mustache. "I may have helped a little," he said, "but mostly it was the passageway."

"What passageway?"

His raised his brows. "The passageway between your homes." He took in their blank expressions. "You might call it… a wormhole?"

"A wormhole. Like on Star Trek? Are you kidding me?"

"A wormhole is real," he said, somewhat petulantly.

"A wormhole is not real. It's a made-up thing in science fiction movies. You can't tell me that they are real."

He scratched his ear and looked at Francesca, who was still holding her phone to her ear and looking at them in shock. Reg shrugged dramatically.

"I'm sorry. Don't ask me. I didn't tell him to transport us. It just happened. I don't know what this nonsense about a wormhole is; I haven't heard anything about it before."

"Not to worry," Francesca said politely. "You are here now, and that means we don't have to wait."

"Right. Do you have any idea where they went? Did you check the attic?"

"I did look this time, in case they got up there again. And I looked for a vent or a hole in the wall that they could have climbed, but I could not find anything. I do not know how they got up there, and I do not know where they went this time."

"Cats can squeeze into some pretty tight places. The kattakyns may not be real kittens, but they are small enough they could get through a pretty small hole."

Francesca shrugged. "You see if you can find any very small holes that they could get through. Can you sense where they are?"

Reg closed her eyes, thinking about it and feeling for Nicole. Last time, Nicole had tried to confuse her to keep her from finding them. This time, Nicole must have gone wherever the kittens had. Reg rubbed her fingers together to get Starlight's attention. He approached her, rubbing against her legs and purring, giving her extra psychic energy to extend the search. Then he drew away from her, sniffing along the ground. Reg watched him.

"Do you know where they are? Can you smell them?"

He continued to move away from her, intent on some scent, and Reg decided it was worth it to go with him and see if he had any luck. They got to a closed door in the kitchen. Reg raised her eyebrows at Francesca.

"A basement?"

"I told you I do not have a basement."

"Then where does that door go?"

Francesca looked at it. "I do not know."

"You don't know where the door goes? You live here. Is it a broom closet?" She reached out and turned the door handle, but the door did not open.

Francesca made a noise that was half-laughing, nearly a sob. "I have never seen that door before," she said. "There was just... a blank panel there."

"Well, now there is a door. It seems like it's stuck."

"Pull harder," Francesca suggested. She reached out and took the door handle in Reg's place. "Just... pull..." She gave it a yank, but it didn't budge. Reg turned around and looked at Harrison. "Can you open this door?"

He looked at it for a moment, then shrugged. He made a flicking gesture, and it shuddered, then opened on its own.

"Uh... thanks. That's a good trick."

Reg pulled the door open the rest of the way. The air smelled moist. There were wooden stairs that descended into the darkness. Reg felt the wall for a light switch, but couldn't find one. She tried to peer into the darkness above her, and moved her hand around, searching for a pull-string, but she couldn't find any way to turn on a light.

"How could they be down here?" Francesca demanded. "How could they get through that door? They cannot open normal doors. They cannot open a door that is stuck or magically sealed."

"I don't know... but something is down there, and we are going to go see what it is."

"You should not tread into darkness without a light," Harrison contributed.

"I've got a light." Reg turned on the flashlight app on her phone and held it in front of her. "Am I going by myself or is someone coming with me?"

* * *

Reg descended the stairs slowly, shining her phone light ahead of her on each one to make sure she wasn't stepping into a dark abyss. The stairs felt spongy beneath her feet, each giving way slightly as she stepped on them. Francesca followed a step or two behind her, grumbling as she went. The kattakyns couldn't be down there. They shouldn't just walk into it without knowing what they were going into. But how were they supposed to know what was down there without looking?

"Are you down here, kitties?" Reg called softly. "Nicole? Kittens? I'm coming down."

The staircase was longer than she expected, more than the thirteen or fourteen steps that she would expect for a typical basement. And they didn't have basements in Florida. So why was there one in Francesca's house? Reg pushed away the anxiety she felt about going underground. She had been able to go underground when they entered the pixie realm; it shouldn't be hard to walk into someone's basement. Even if it were just a dirt floor, what was she going to find that would be so terrible? Skeletons? Rats? If the cats had retreated to the basement, then she wouldn't have to worry about rats. And she was quite sure she wasn't going to find any skeletons. That kind of thing didn't happen in real life.

Ghosts?

There certainly might be ghosts, but that would be nothing new for Reg. They couldn't do anything to scare her. No more than Norma Jean could. She was the scariest spirit that Reg could remember.

Finally, Reg's feet hit the floor. It was concrete rather than packed earth. Everything was damp, as she had expected. She shone the phone light around the large room. It didn't penetrate far into the darkness, but there wasn't much to see. The room was almost entirely empty.

"Nicole!" Francesca saw the cat's shining eyes in the darkness and moved past Reg. "You are a naughty kitty! You quit trying to hide the kittens! I don't know how you got down here, but you just stop it! It scares me when I cannot find you!"

Francesca moved into the room and shooed the cats toward the stairs. Reg felt their disappointment at being found and resignation at going back upstairs to the main part of the house. Francesca had said before that cats needed to roam outside, and Reg was sure that in this case, Francesca was right. The cats would have gone outside if they could have. They didn't want to be cooped up in the house. They wanted to get away before Francesca could split them up.

Starlight meowed. Reg looked at him, startled. She hadn't realized that he had followed her down the stairs. He was looking at her, his ears standing up in attention, whiskers bristling with curiosity. Reg looked around. She was surprised that he hadn't gone upstairs with Nicole. He always loved being around Nicole. But he seemed to be more interested in the basement this time. Maybe there had been rats, and he could still smell them. All Reg could smell was dampness.

She walked around the room, shining her light along the wall and into each dark corner. The basement was undeveloped. Reg had expected some dusty old preserves lining a few old storage shelves. Unlike some of the homes she had lived in farther north, there was no furnace in the basement. Under the stairs, there was another closed door—a little storage closet. Probably filled with old brooms and spiders.

Reg grasped the handle and tried to turn it, but unlike the hidden door at the top of the stairs, the handle did not turn. It was locked. Reg looked around for the others. Francesca was shooing the cats up the stairs. Harrison hadn't followed them down. It was just Reg and Starlight. She tried the door once more, but it didn't budge.

"Well, I guess that's it," Reg told Starlight.

He looked at her. He sniffed along the bottom of the door and then pawed at it. He clearly wanted her to open it, but Reg could not comply. She tried to imagine the inner workings of the lock to see if she could persuade it to unlock. Since being locked up in the warehouse with Corvin and Warren and the others, she had been attempting to manipulate locks with her mind. It hadn't worked in the warehouse because there had been a spell on the locks. But she had been able to open some of the locks she had tried at home.

The lock to the closet resisted her efforts and she wasn't able to get it open. She walked back up the stairs, Starlight trailing behind her. When they reached the kitchen, he sat down and started washing. Reg imagined that if she had to walk through the basement barefoot, she would have wanted to clean her feet off too. They were probably caked with dust and cobwebs.

Francesca was trying to count up the cats to make sure that all ten were there. Harrison had either disappeared or was in another part of the house. Reg wasn't sure how she was going to get back home. Maybe a cab.

"Do you have a key to the closet down there?" she asked Francesca.

"What closet?"

"There is one under the stairs."

"I did not see a closet," Francesca said dismissively.

"Well, you didn't go through the whole basement. It was under the stairs; you had to go around and under…"

"I do not have a key for any door."

"What about the door to the house? Maybe it would fit? Or maybe there were some keys left here by the previous owner, on a peg or in a junk drawer?"

Francesca hesitated, then nodded. She opened the drawer closest to the back door. She picked through it, taking out a few random keys on rings. Sometimes there were two or three keys on one ring, sometimes just one. There were a few that were obviously for padlocks, too small for a door lock. Reg looked through the remaining keys.

"It could be any of these."

She went to the basement door and again went down the stairs carefully, using her phone as a flashlight. She went around the stairs to the little cubby underneath, and stopped, staring at a blank wall. "What the…"

She felt along it, looking for a panel or crack. There had been a door. A doorknob with a lock. But there was no longer any sign of it.

"What's going on here?"

She closed her eyes and tried to picture it in her mind. She knew where it had been. She drew the lines out in her mind, glowing bright lines around the crack in the door. A bright door handle. She reached out and grasped it. She could feel the knob in her hand. It was warm and rough. But it was still locked. She opened her eyes and could see nothing but the faint afterimage of the light. She was still holding on to the doorknob, but it wasn't there. She felt for the keyhole and, keeping track of it with one hand, brought the first of the orphaned keys out and tried to fit it into the hole. It didn't go in. She went methodically through each one of them, but couldn't force any of them into the hole. They were all wrong.

Or she couldn't fit them into the keyhole because there actually wasn't a doorknob with a keyhole there.

Reg went through each key again. She could feel the cutaway of the keyhole, but she couldn't fit any of the keys into it.

Finally, she turned and went back up the stairs.

"You see?" Francesca said immediately. "There is no door down there."

"There is a door, but it's gone invisible again. I could still feel the door handle, but I can't fit any of the keys into it."

Francesca lifted one eyebrow in disbelief. She probably thought Reg was making up those details to cover up the fact that there was, in fact, no door in the basement. Reg put her hands on her hips.

"There is a door!"

"I did not see a door. Perhaps you are right… but perhaps you are not."

"Just because you can't see a thing, that doesn't mean it doesn't exist."

"That is true," Francesca admitted. "But it is not usually the case with a door."

"You never saw this door before." Reg pointed at the door leading to the basement. "So why don't you believe there's another door you can't see?"

"I can see this one. I just never noticed it before," Francesca said, revising her previous recollection. Reg had seen that reaction before. When something was impossible to believe, the person simply made up an explanation that they could believe. They replaced the memory, and then the world made sense again. Reg didn't like to think of how many times she might have done that herself. There had been a lot of things in her previous life that hadn't made any sense. How many memories had she replaced in order to keep her sanity?

Francesca closed the basement door. As she did so, it disappeared into the paneling. Reg stepped forward, trying to grab the door handle and open it again. "You can't do that! Don't shut it!"

But she was protesting far too late. Francesca had already closed it, and they were both left to stare at the blank panel. "You see," Francesca pointed out. "It's just because it blends in so well."

"It's gone!" Reg felt for the door handle, but couldn't find it.

"The cats are back, so everything is fine," Francesca pointed out. She wasn't going to be deterred by missing doors. Her only concern was with the cats, and now that they had been found again, she could forget about any inconvenient wormholes or disappearing doorways. Reg looked around, wanting to ask Harrison whether there was any relationship between the doors and the wormhole. Maybe they had come in through the door, and that was why it had become visible. Or maybe it had been Harrison's presence, or he had worked some magic to make it appear so that they could find the kittens. He loved cats, after all; it followed that he would do whatever was necessary to make sure they were found and kept safe.

He wasn't in the kitchen. Reg went into the living room and found him sitting on the floor, the cats surrounding him and crawling over him. He was giggling like a toddler. Starlight and Nicole were nearby, rubbing against and grooming each other and watching the strange man play with the kittens.

"Harrison."

It took a couple of times before Reg was able to get his attention. Harrison looked up. "Oh, Regina. Did you find what you were looking for?"

He was playing with the cats, so obviously he knew she had found them. Reg shook her head, brushing away the question. "Can you help with the door? It has disappeared again."

"You must open it to see it," Harrison advised.

Reg stared at him, willing him to say something sane. She had to open it to see it? She had opened it, but she had been able to see it before that. She could not open it if she couldn't see it. He was getting it backward.

"I've tried. I can't see it. I can't feel it. I want to get back to the basement. There is another door down there. A closet. I want to see what's in it." That didn't fully express what she was feeling. "I *need* to see what's in it."

"The door does not belong to you."

"No. I know that. It's Francesca's. But she didn't do anything to make it appear or disappear."

Except to close it. Maybe she was more than a charmer. Maybe she had some pretty sophisticated magic that allowed her to manipulate those doors and to hide them when necessary. She had some secret to hide and didn't want Reg to see it.

"It is not Francesca's door either."

"It's in her house."

"It is not her door."

Reg shook her head. "Okay. Then how do I get it to appear again?"

"You need all of the keys."

"I have the keys." Reg held up the keys from the drawer in the kitchen.

"Humans are so charmingly literal."

Reg blew out her breath in frustration. "Tell me what I need to do to see the door again. And I might need you to open it like you did last time. Then I want to be able to see the one downstairs too. And to unlock it so I can see what is in the closet."

"You got it right the first time. Use your tools, Regina. You have been given everything you need." Harrison held a kitten on either side of his face, cooing at them and making silly faces.

Reg didn't know how she was supposed to take him seriously when he behaved like a fool.

She had been given everything she needed. What had been different when she'd walked up to the door the first time?

She had been following Starlight. He had led her to each of the doors.

"Starlight. I need you. Let's go look at the doors again."

Starlight was busy with his lady friend and did not even flick a whisker in Reg's direction.

"Come on, Star. Don't you want to see what's in the closet? You were trying to get in there. Let's go see."

He still didn't pay her any attention. Usually, when Reg needed help with a psychic project, he was quick to come when called. It was the only time he did. But he was too distracted by Nicole to pay her any mind. Nicole was, once again, throwing up barriers in Reg's way. Why did she care whether Reg opened the closet or not? She had been down there with the kittens, so she had, in effect, led Reg to the closet.

Reg marched over to where Starlight and Nicole were grooming and picked Starlight up.

He gave a startled squawk and tried to twist around to right himself. Reg let him turn himself right-side up, but wouldn't let him go. He kicked with his strong back legs, giving her a long scratch down one arm.

"Ouch! Stop it!"

Starlight stopped kicking. He looked at Reg reproachfully.

"Don't look at me like that; you hurt me! And you're not listening to me. You're my familiar. You're supposed to help me at least when I ask you to help with a job like this. Even if you don't pay any attention to me the rest of the time."

He was still in her arms. Reg walked with him into the kitchen and stood in front of the blank panel where the door had been. And there it was, just as it had been before. Reg rolled her eyes. "This is getting ridiculous. Doors shouldn't appear and disappear. So why do I need you to see the door?"

Reg knew that the first time, turning the handle hadn't worked. Harrison's magic had been required to make it open. But Reg had some of those powers herself. If her father was Weston, who knew what powers she had inherited from him?

She focused on the doorknob, feeling inside it. The doorknob itself wasn't locked. The door had just stuck. Magically sealed. Until someone who knew the right magic could open it.

She mentally ran her attention all the way around the door, making sure that it was free of the frame.

Open.

As when they had asked Harrison to help with the door, it simply creaked open.

"There, you see?" Reg asked Starlight. "Just a little bit of the right kind of attention, and it opens all by itself."

Reg put Starlight down at the top of the stairs. "Now, are you going to go down with me and see if we can get the door open?"

He stood there, sniffing the air from the basement. He looked up at her.

"Are we going to do this? Harrison said that we have what we need to open the door. I don't know why I need you, but apparently, I do. So let's go down together and see what's in that closet."

Whatever was in the closet, it didn't belong to Francesca. Not unless her ignorance of the basement and the closet was an act, and Reg was pretty good at discerning when someone was lying. She didn't think that Francesca had anything to do with the appearing and disappearing doors. Or at least, not intentionally. Whatever was behind that door, it was Reg's.

Starlight started to descend the stairs, placing his paws carefully on each step. Reg took his lead and was also careful not to trip or to stay on any one stair for too long. Who knew how rotten they were?

They walked around the stairs again to the place where the closet door had been the first time.

And there it was. Reg didn't need her psychic powers to see it or to remember where it was. She again tried the random keys in the keyhole, even though she knew none of them had fit before. Maybe they would now that the door was visible. It was, at least, easier to try them.

Again, none of the keys fit. Starlight prowled along the bottom of the door, sniffing it and scratching at it.

"I'm doing the best I can," Reg told him.

He sat back and looked at her as if waiting for her to get

herself together and figure it out. Reg raised her eyebrows. "What? Exactly what do you expect me to do about it? I need the key. Without the key, I can't get in."

Harrison had told her that she had the key and that she could unlock it. So why couldn't she?

CHAPTER TWENTY-ONE

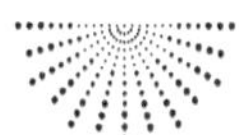

$\mathcal{I}$t was as if she had been resisting putting the puzzle together until then. She knew very well what the answer was, but she hadn't been able to make the connection. She reached into her skirt pocket and drew out the key that Forst had found in the garden. *She had a key.* She had been trying to find the lock for it so that they could claim her treasure. Now she was presented with a lock without a key, and she hadn't made the connection.

"Do you think this is it?" Reg asked Starlight. She held the key up. "Is it that simple? The key was in the cottage garden; there is a wormhole from the cottage to here. There is a locked closet here."

On the one hand, she was disappointed. She had been hoping for a treasure chest, sarcophagus, or some other proper receptacle for a treasure. But a basement under-stairs cubby? What treasure was she going to find there?

There was no reason it couldn't hide a trove of gold bars, jewels, or some other priceless treasure. But it seemed highly unlikely. Probably it was nothing but dust and spiders. And a broom. Maybe she could ride the broom home if Harrison didn't want to transport her again or the wormhole had mysteriously closed.

Reg held the key in the palm of her hand for a few more seconds. It was warm, and the familiar tug was stronger than ever. It wanted to be reunited with the lock. That was its purpose.

She reoriented the key and slid it into the lock. Unlike the other keys, which didn't even fit into the slot, let alone turn the tumblers, it fit neatly into place. Reg held her breath. She looked at Starlight, then twisted the key.

There was no explosion or magical spell. Reg turned the handle. It was now unlocked. She pulled the closet door open.

The magical phenomenon she had expected when she had turned the key blasted into the basement. Light seared Reg's eyeballs after the darkness of the basement. It exploded out of the closet and lit up the room like midday. She couldn't look into the closet; it was far too bright.

"What is it?" she asked aloud.

"It's about time," a male voice boomed.

The light coalesced into a single form but was still too bright to look at.

The basement disappeared, and Reg and Starlight were, once again, in the living room with Harrison, Nicole, and the kittens. But this time, there was another man too.

He was tall like Harrison, but fuller in the chest, a huskier build. He didn't have a mustache and looked vaguely like the lumberjack in a TV commercial—handsome, rugged, and glowing from inside.

He looked around at each of them, his eyes bright and intelligent. His eyes pinned Reg down. "It is you?" he asked. "You are the child?"

Reg looked at him uncertainly. She diverted her gaze to Harrison, looking for help.

"She is the child," Harrison agreed. "We expected you to be near the woman."

The man ignored the comment. He looked at Starlight. Then his eyes moved to the kittens and he started to laugh.

It was a deep belly laugh that shook his whole body and brought tears to the corners of his eyes.

"Destine, Destine! What have you done?"

Reg smiled a little. He obviously recognized his old enemy, even without a proper physical form and with his consciousness divided through the nine kattakyns. She tried to get his attention again.

"Are you… Weston?"

His lips curled upward. "Of course. Who were you expecting?"

"I don't know that I was expecting a who… I was expecting more of a what."

"A hidden treasure?" he suggested. He laughed heartily. "What treasure could be better than releasing me from my prison?"

Reg was still trying to wrap her mind around what had happened. "So all of this was intentional? Planned? Me moving here and finding the key? Starlight and Nicole? The wormhole from the cottage to this house?"

Weston shrugged. "Human intelligence is limited," he told her condescendingly. "You are not expected to understand how it works."

"Well… thanks for that, but I think I can actually sort it out." Even though the magnitude of what he had done was beyond her grasp. How could he have known where she would go, who she would develop friendships with, how the key would fall into her possession and eventually lead her to find and unlock the hidden doors?

Weston watched the kittens, chortling again, but quietly this time.

Starlight picked his way over to Weston delicately, as if tiptoeing through water. He sat at Weston's feet and drew himself up tall.

"Ah, my old friend," Weston said. He made a noise in the back of his throat, then bent over to pick Starlight up. Starlight rubbed against the bottom of Weston's chin, purring.

Reg watched the interaction between Weston and Starlight with a certain amount of jealousy. What was the deal with the immortals and cats, and Starlight in particular? Was he indeed the reincarnation of another immortal or a human whom Harrison and Weston had known in a past life? Or was he that long-lived? Cats weren't supposed to live for more than fifteen or twenty years. How could someone who had been banished or bound for thirty years or more know him?

And more than that, why wasn't Weston paying Reg any attention? If she was his long-lost daughter, shouldn't he be happy to see her? Maybe a hug or a declaration of love? If not for her, then maybe a word for Norma Jean, the lover he had lost? It was as if she were some tool that, once used, he was now ready to discard.

"If you're Weston, then does that mean you're my father?" she demanded.

Weston looked at her as if surprised to hear her speak. "How long has it been?" he asked Harrison. "In human years?"

"Longer than one would expect, maybe, but less than a century."

"Thirty years," Reg answered. "I am thirty years old. And if you left when I was four, it has been twenty-six years."

"Four what?" Weston asked with a frown of concentration. "Four orbits? You were not so much. Still in the woman's belly."

"You left with Norma Jean pregnant with me? You never even saw me after I was born?"

She could hear Norma Jean's agreement in her head. He had left her, abandoned her pregnant and alone, without any resources. Just like a man.

"Waiting four years, the others would surely have found me and dealt with me. Destine especially." Weston chuckled, looking at the kittens. "He used to be a threat."

"I know. We had to face him."

"You?"

"Me and my friends. Humans. Since the immortals would not help us out."

"Brought so low by humans. *Oh, Destine!*"

"Aren't you listening to me?" Reg said. "You abandoned Norma Jean. You abandoned me. I didn't live an easy life. Destine killed Norma Jean! Tortured her to death when she couldn't tell him where you were. And me and my friends had to confront him and defeat him. Humans facing a powerful immortal. Don't you have anything to say about that?"

He stared at her blankly for a few seconds in silence. Then he shrugged. "You did well," he said eventually. "You must have strong gifts."

"I don't know what gifts I have, how strong they are. I have been trying to understand what they were and where they came from. I don't know how… what I have."

Weston petted Starlight thoughtfully. He eventually put the cat down, giving him one last scratch behind the ears.

"Continue to guide her. We will talk."

And then he was gone. No poof of smoke or other drama, he was just there one instant, and then he was not. Reg looked around the room. She didn't know whether his words had been directed at Starlight or Harrison. She had no idea where he had gone. She looked at Harrison, confused, looking for his direction.

"What was that all about? Where did he go?"

Harrison pursed his lips, looking at her. "Are you sure it was such a good idea to release him?"

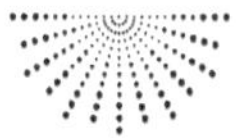

$\mathcal{R}$eg looked at Harrison, her mouth dropping open in disbelief. "Do you think that I released him on purpose? I had no idea that was what was in the closet. I thought… maybe there was something valuable there. I didn't know it was Weston! Did *you* know?"

He shrugged. "That was the most likely outcome."

"Why didn't you tell me?"

"I assumed you knew."

"How would I know?"

Harrison's brows lowered slightly as he thought about it. "This is where the breadcrumbs led," he said slowly. "Didn't you know they would lead to him?"

Reg dug the sharp knuckles of her fist into her forehead, trying to fend off the headache starting between her eyes. "I didn't know! Why didn't you say something to me? If you had told me, then I would have been able to make an informed choice!"

"I told you that you came here because of him. That you could feel his imprint here. I told you that the path led from your house to this. I told you that you had the keys to open the door." He shook his head. "I did tell you, Reg."

"You need to… not assume that I know what you mean. You

need to tell me clearly, like we're talking right now. Tell me 'Weston is probably in the closet and if you use the key to open it, you will release him.'"

Harrison scratched an eyebrow, then nodded. He curled his mustache around his index fingers and released the ends again. "Weston is probably in the closet—" he started out.

"It's too late now; I already let him out!"

"Well, yes."

"You were supposed to tell me that before I let him out."

"To be fair, you didn't tell me that until after."

Reg growled in frustration. Harrison scratched the back of his neck. "There is a problem."

"What?"

"When Weston was previously free… his power was balanced by Destine's."

"Yeah?"

"But now…" Harrison fluttered his fingers at the cats. "Destine's power has been divided. And most of it consumed by your spirit-eater."

"He's not *my* spirit-eater."

Harrison shrugged, his expression doubtful. "But he is."

"He took most of the Witch Doctor's powers," Reg attempted to move on from the argument about whether Corvin was hers or not. "All except what the Witch Doctor was able to retain when he went into the draugrs. So what does that mean? Corvin needs to fight Weston?"

"They do not need to fight… as long as their powers are balanced."

"Okay… what then? What does he need to do?"

"Perhaps, as you said, we should tell him directly."

"Yeah, we probably—"

Reg blinked at Corvin, standing in front of her. He stared back at her. He had a stick razor in his hand, held close to his face as he leaned forward. There was shaving cream layered thickly over his face like a banana cream pie.

Corvin straightened up and looked around the room. His eyes took in Reg, Harrison, and the cats. Looking through the doorway, Reg could still see Francesca in the kitchen. She clearly did not want anything to do with the drama Reg and Harrison were in the midst of.

"Regina…" Corvin greeted. "Nice to see you again…"

"I'm sorry. It wasn't my idea. He just… poofed you here."

"I see."

"Your power is great," Harrison observed. "But you do not yet have it under control. You struggle to master it."

Corvin darted a look at Harrison, then shook his head at Reg, his eyes indicating his confusion.

"It's… it's about Weston," Reg said.

"Do we now know exactly who Weston is?"

"Um… I guess he was my father. An immortal. He was bound. And now… he is free again."

"Regina released him," Harrison contributed helpfully.

"Uh… yeah. I guess I did. But it wasn't intentional. It would have helped if someone had given me all of the information. If someone knew how to give a straight answer to a question."

"Someone did not," Harrison agreed with a sober nod of agreement.

Corvin's eyebrows were up as he tried to take all of this in and get caught up on what was going on. "Okay, then. You've released an immortal from his exile. I assume that's going to be a problem."

"His power is no longer opposed," Harrison explained. "When he was last loose, he was counterbalanced by Destine. But since your defeat of Destine…"

"He is no longer in the equation," Corvin contributed.

Harrison was nodding.

"But wait a minute," Reg interrupted. "If the Witch Doctor was the evil force, and he counterbalanced Weston, then Weston is the good guy, and if the Witch Doctor is not opposing him, that is a good thing, not a bad thing. He can… do good without worrying about being stopped by the Witch Doctor. Isn't that right?"

"Mmm…" Harrison pursed his lips and shook his head slowly. "No, that is not right."

Reg sighed in exasperation. "Why not? Doesn't that make sense?"

"It is not a matter of good and bad," Corvin said. "I think that rather, it is an issue of having absolute power. You've heard the expression that power corrupts, and absolute power corrupts absolutely."

"You're afraid he is going to take over the world?" Reg put the question to Harrison. "Is that what you're talking about?"

Harrison looked down at her. "Humans do have strange ideas of their importance in the universe."

"Explain to me what he is going to do, then."

Harrison stared at her for a moment, then looked at Corvin. "In some cases, words do not suffice," he said helplessly. "We will go to him."

Before Reg could protest or could prepare herself, the room changed around them. Instead of being in Francesca's living room, they were in a tiny, foul-smelling apartment. Little more than a flop house, it was covered with filth, the walls spattered and stained with unidentifiable matter, garbage on the floor, and the smell of rats permeating the air.

"Where are we?" Corvin asked softly.

There was a hard knot of iron in Reg's stomach. "I think… I don't know. Please get us out of here," she begged.

Corvin gave her an odd look. Reg pressed her knuckle into her teeth. She did not want to be there. It wasn't fair of Harrison to bring her there. Or for Weston to be there. He had run away. He had not stayed around to see her born or to protect her or Norma Jean. He had disappeared and had not been a part of either of their lives.

But now Norma Jean sat on one of the chairs, giggling and talking animatedly. The person that she was talking to was

Weston. He leaned over her attentively, a big smile on his face, treating her as if she were a princess.

Norma Jean was missing teeth, and what she still had were rotting. Her hair was brittle and falling out. She was not the lovely lady she claimed to have been when she left her home as a teenager to start a life on her own. The streets had seen to her quick decline and the loss of her youth, beauty, and health. Reg didn't understand why Weston was treating her as if she still had those things. Maybe in his eyes, she was something different. Perhaps he could see her the way that she had been.

"This is wrong," Reg said anxiously. She could no longer hear Norma Jean's voice in her head. Norma Jean had been a resident there for so long that Reg wasn't sure what to do without her there. Had Norma Jean been returned to life? Was that what Weston had done?

"Her name is Regina," Norma Jean was saying to Weston, not inside Regina's head, but outside of it. "She is just a little thing. You have to meet her."

"No," Regina protested. "No, this isn't right. Norma Jean is dead. This isn't happening."

"I don't know if this really is happening," Corvin cautioned. "It might just be a vision…"

"She is really there. She isn't inside of me anymore. She's alive. That can't be. Did we go back in time?" Regina looked around the room, trying to remember the place she had lived before going into foster care. She had been so young. She looked around, shaking her head, trying to match it to the imprint in her brain.

"Where is she?" Norma Jean asked, her voice growing more strident. "Are you hiding again, you silly girl? She's always squeezing into the smallest spaces, hiding away like a mouse."

Weston straightened up. He walked confidently across the apartment to the kitchenette. There wasn't a separate kitchen, no separate food preparation or eating area. More like a hotel room, just a few cupboards and a counter for a hot plate. Reg hugged herself tightly.

"No," she protested, "no, no, no!"

Weston opened one of the lower cupboard doors. Regina saw the pale, dirty little red-haired girl pressed into the corner. The child covered her face as if that would keep Weston from seeing her. Weston reached down and wrapped his long fingers around her body, picking her up. She was a tiny waif of a thing; it took no effort for him to lift her.

"Stop. You need to stop him! This isn't right. This isn't the way it happened."

"If you don't change things, this is the way it happened," Harrison said.

"That doesn't make any sense! This isn't what happened. You protected me. You made it so that the Witch Doctor couldn't find me."

"The Witch Doctor is no longer here," Harrison explained. "That means that Weston could come. He could see you and affect the course of your life."

"No! He wasn't here. He abandoned us." Reg was frantic. They had to stop Weston from changing everything.

"Isn't this what you want?" Corvin asked as he scraped the shaving cream from his face into the sink. "Don't you want him to protect you and your mother?"

Reg pressed her fingers to her temples. How many times over the years had she dreamed of being rescued by her father or by anyone? She had longed for someone to appear in her life and whisk her away to safety. She even prayed for her mother to be returned to life so that she could go back to a stable home and not have to be shuffled from place to place in foster care. Now, if she were to believe Harrison, that could all change. The past could be changed. Weston could rescue them and she could have what she'd always wished for.

But what would that mean?

If Reg stayed with Norma Jean instead of going into foster care, would Reg still be the same person? Would she be wiping out her entire existence? And would staying with Norma Jean be better than foster care? She'd had to deal with a lot of disruption and abuse in foster care, but she knew Norma Jean was just as abusive. Reg would live in abject poverty, moving from flophouse to shelter to sleeping rough on the street. There had been good foster homes, parents who had tried their best to give her what she needed and help her to heal the wounds of the past, even if Reg had always proven to be too difficult a case and had not been able to stay anywhere long-term. There had been therapists and specialists and even hospitalization. Staying with Norma Jean would have meant losing all of those supports.

Staying with Norma Jean would not have been an idyllic life. Norma Jean had just been her first, most traumatic loss, the one from which she had always been trying to recover.

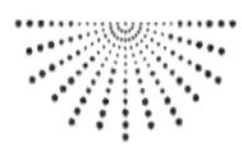

"Mommy," Reg whispered, her throat tight, realizing she was going to have to lose Norma Jean again, and this time it would be her own choice.

She grasped Corvin's arm, drawing strength from him. "We have to stop this. He can't be allowed to change everything."

At first, he tried to pull out of her grasp, then he let her hang on to him. "I don't know how you do that," he muttered.

"What?" Reg was focused on Weston, not Corvin, trying to figure out how best to deter him.

"Draw on my powers."

"If we work together, we can defeat him, can't we?" Reg asked desperately. She looked at Harrison. "Tell me we can."

Harrison shrugged. He looked interested, but not overly concerned.

"That's why you brought us here. You said that Corvin could balance out his power."

"If he can *control* his powers," Harrison said, doubt in his tone.

Reg tightened her grip on Corvin's arm, seeking the warmth and energy he held, drawing on it. "Weston! Put the girl down! You need to leave them alone."

Her voice didn't come out nearly as authoritatively as she wanted it to, but it was the best she could do, with her throat constricted and her knees shaking. Weston didn't even look at her, still talking to Norma Jean and tickling the little girl under the chin like a cat.

"Weston!"

He turned and looked at her, then glanced over at Harrison and raised his eyebrows. "There is no need to bring so many people to this family reunion. It is just my dear one and me and the child."

"You can't have her. You aren't allowed to do this. That's why you were bound."

"I have served my exile and been released. You cannot punish me a second time." He gave a little laugh. "You could not punish me anyway."

"We have the power of the Witch Doctor—of Destine!" Reg told him shakily. "You can't just do whatever you want without consequence."

"Indeed." Weston studied Corvin move closely, taking a step toward them. "How could this spirit-drinker best Samyr Destine? Unless it was his time. Did he grow careless? Or had he run his course?" he mused, not directing the question at any of them.

"Let the little girl go," Corvin commanded, his voice sounding much more commanding than Reg's. "You are not allowed to be here."

"I am not allowed? I am immortal; I go where I like. There is nothing to stop me from being here."

"You are not supposed to have contact with the woman or the child. You broke the rules. I am here to stop you."

Corvin was bluffing pretty well, considering how little he knew. But he probably had a little more background knowledge on the immortals than he would disclose. He had pretended only to have a general understanding of them, but he seemed to be up-to-date on the rules on not having children with the mortals. Or had Reg told him that?

Her head was hurting like it was going to split right down the middle. If she were anywhere else, she would have lain down to go to sleep. Her brain was shutting down with the pain and the confusion over what she was supposed to do and how she could possibly influence what had happened in her past. Or maybe it was just a side effect of traveling through time.

Maybe she was having a stroke, and none of it was happening after all. It was just a very vivid dream caused by the damage spreading through her brain. She would be seeing the light at the end of a tunnel soon and meeting all of her loved ones who had gone on before.

Or maybe Norma Jean was the only one she would ever meet. The only one she had ever loved, in spite of the way Norma Jean had treated her.

"*I am,*" Weston said thunderously. "You have no control over me. The others have no control over me. I have paid the price and I can now choose my own path without retribution."

"No!" Reg insisted. She lunged at Weston, letting go of Corvin, her source of strength. "Not if I have anything to say about it!"

Weston was startled by her attack, merely buffeting her with the back of his arm to keep her away from him, not casting any spell or using his immortal powers. Reg immediately renewed her attack. She needed to stop him. To get the child away from him and prevent him from changing everything. The child could not stay with Norma Jean. Weston could not protect the two of them. The results would be disastrous. She grabbed ahold of Weston this time, not letting him simply smack her back again. She grabbed his fingers and bent them back, attempting to pry the little girl away from him.

"Let her go! Her fate isn't yours to choose. You already made your decision; you can't go back and change it now. She has to grow up like I did."

The little girl was cowering away from Reg. She hid her face against the strange man in an attempt to escape the scary, screaming, wild-eyed woman. She was starting to sob, but held back, trying to keep them from seeing her tears. How many times had she been punished for crying?

Weston attempted to shove Reg back again, but she threw up the wall around herself so that he couldn't touch her. She yelled, an incoherent war-cry. She was the protector of this child. She had to keep him from messing everything up. If he did what he planned, he would only hurt her more. Reg drew on the powers that Corvin held. They were no longer touching physically, but she had left a path open to him, and when she directed her thoughts back to him, there was an immediate connection. They worked together in sync as if they had practiced this scene a thousand times. Each knew what the other was going to do the instant before it happened.

Reg tried to force the child from Weston's arms. To begin with, he only resisted physically. Perhaps his powers were rusty after all of his time in the closet. Or maybe he didn't believe that she could hold any power that would challenge him.

But as he struggled with her, he started to put up a magical resistance as well. Reg had to work harder and harder to keep her hands on the little girl and to even stand in front of the immortal. He tried to hit or push her, but the wall that she had put up protected her from physical harm. He started attacking her psychic forces, the power that she was drawing from Corvin.

She felt him stirring inside her mind and tried to fight back and push him out. How could it be so easy for him to get behind her defenses? He stirred up old memories.

Reg, cuddling in Norma Jean's arms as her mother rocked her, sitting in a rocking chair in a hospital or shelter somewhere, not in the dirty little apartment. Little Reg was warm and felt protected. She didn't understand the words of the song that her mother sang to her as she relaxed and tried to find a peaceful sleep without dreams. She didn't have any idea, as the Reg of older years did, that rather than a lullaby, it was a drinking song, normally raucous and rowdy.

Then she felt Harrison's warm protection spell as she hid in the cupboard, but then the terror of watching her mother being tortured.

And then the horrible sense of being alone in the world, ricocheting from one place to another as they searched for a home that could manage her, promising that she would have a forever family who would take care of her and keep her safe forever if she would just be good—knowing that she never could be.

Reg could barely hold on to consciousness, faltering in her attempts to fight back against Weston. He picked and chose the memories that would weaken her, that would best convince her to leave the child with him and Norma Jean. Together, they could be the perfect little family. He could protect her from every negative force in the world. He could keep her safe at all times. He could be the loving father she'd never had. He would see to it that she had food to eat and was warm and safely tucked into bed each night.

"Regina!" Corvin tried to shake her from her stupor. "Reg, fight! Don't let him get to you. You don't *want* him to protect you. He never will, anyway. You know what these immortals are like. They have great ideas, how they're going to change the world and make it a better place, and instead, they end up destroying civilizations or leading countries into war and then wandering off when they get bored with it. He wouldn't have stayed with you. He would have taken off after the next shiny new idea."

It was true. Reg renewed her attempts to fight against him and against the memories he endeavored to drown her with. She could not let him lull her into a sense of security. Those warm fuzzy feelings weren't true. He hadn't been there her whole life, and even if he intended to protect the child, he would never follow through. He would always be chasing after a new woman, idea, or treasure. The immortals were fickle.

Even Harrison, her trusty, helpful Uncle Harrison, who had promised he would always be there to help and protect her had disappeared more times than she could count. Had he stayed near her to ensure that the Witch Doctor could never harm her? On the contrary, time after time, he had left her alone, making her vulnerable.

And when he had known that she was getting close to opening the closet and releasing Weston from his imprisonment, he hadn't warned her. He'd just stood by and let it happen.

"You get out of my head and out of my life forever!" Reg shouted so loudly it hurt. "She is not yours!"

"She *is* mine," Weston argued, sounding angry and dangerous for the first time. "She is my blood! I gave her to Norma Jean. She will always be mine."

"No. You gave that up when you abandoned her. You cannot have her!"

"Her power is my power," Weston's voice was low and gravelly. "Your power is my power. You have nothing you can use against me because I am the source!"

Reg was shaken, but she continued to fight back against him. She didn't just have her own gifts to draw on. She was also using Corvin's. And his came from the Witch Doctor, not from Weston. Destine held the power that had counterbalanced Weston for years. Maybe for epochs. They could continue to fight him all day long; Weston couldn't get the upper hand. There was a balance of forces.

Reg held him off, but she couldn't make any progress.

Maybe she could go no farther. Her power combined with Corvin's was not enough to get the upper hand. Reg stared at the little girl. She had to do it for her younger self. She had to do it to protect the little girl from all that would happen to her if Weston succeeded in changing the course of her life.

That little girl was her, and that little girl had the powers that Reg would eventually wield. It didn't make any sense that together they could hold any more than Reg did by herself, but nothing was working the way she thought it should after years of watching Star Trek.

"Look at me, Reg," she said softly, trying to meet her eyes and to smile at her encouragingly. "I know what to do. You can help me. You can help me to protect you."

The little girl looked away, frightened. Reg swallowed. The little girl had never been told she could do anything. How could Reg explain to her what powers she had? Powers that she wouldn't understand for years. Reg was still trying to wrap her mind around them.

Reg's hands were still on the little girl, trying to pull her away from Weston. She relaxed her grip to make sure it didn't hurt. To convey a sense of concern to the girl so she wouldn't be scared. She reached out with her mind and attempted to touch the little girl's inner self. It wasn't truly an invasion of her mind if it was into her own head.

There was a blast of brilliance like she had never experienced before. The little girl's mind was so bright and alive with light and color it just about knocked Reg over. She let out her breath in a puff like she'd been punched in the stomach.

"Whoa!"

The little version of herself looked back with guileless innocence. She cocked her head to the side slightly, trying to figure out who Reg was and what she was doing. Reg couldn't explain, but she tried to show her how to push back against Weston, how to resist him and to build a wall around herself, Reg, and Corvin. She drew on Corvin's strength and funneled it toward the little girl. Corvin sensed what she was doing, and after an initial tug of resistance, he did the best he could to help. But Reg could feel his reluctance. He had battled with an immortal before, and when he had done that, he had been able to pull powers from him. He was hungering again, tugging here and there like a dog on a leash, drawn toward the powers Weston wielded.

"Don't," Reg told him. "Last time, you had just filled up with power from the artifacts. It's different this time."

Corvin spoke through gritted teeth. "I can. I am strong enough."

"Harrison said you don't have control yet."

"He's wrong. I can do this. I did it before without his help."

Reg was losing her grip on the little girl's mind and had to refocus her attention. "Come on, honey. You can do this. You're strong. Wow, all of that power inside of you, you're like a magical princess!"

The little girl's face lit up at this suggestion and, in spite of the dirt on her face and the hollowness of her cheeks, she glowed, exuding light, her power flow amping up noticeably.

Weston's physical grip on the little girl slackened. Reg was able to tug her out of his hands. She held the waif against her body, the desire to protect her welling up even more strongly inside her. She wanted to hold this little girl and protect her from all of the trouble that was going to come to her. But she wasn't going to be there for her.

Or she was, but not with the knowledge and power that she would gain later in life. The little girl could rely only on what was inside her as a four-year-old. Reg kissed her cheek and tried to pump her up as much as she could inside her mind. She told her how brave and strong she was and that she was beautiful and smart no matter what anyone else told her. And there would be people there for her. Uncle Harrison sometimes, and social workers and doctors and foster parents who really did care and wanted to do the best for her. The bad times would only be temporary. She would be able to get through them.

The girl clung to her neck. Reg turned her attention back to Weston and built a spell against him.

"You can't have her. She is not yours; she is her own person. You stay away from her."

"She is my blood!"

"It doesn't matter. That doesn't mean you possess her. Humans are independent. You leave her alone."

"I can make her great. I can build her powers, teach her how to use her gifts and talents properly. By the time she is grown, she will be a sorceress beyond description. Think of having that kind of power. Think of how different your life would be."

It was a temptation, as Weston knew it would be. She had always struggled for control. She hadn't cared so much about having power over other people as just having the right to make her own choices and not have her life run by all of the adults.

But that was what had made her the person she was.

"No. That's not what she needs."

"Of course she does. It's what you always wanted. Do you think I can't see that?"

In wrestling with him, however much she had tried to build a wall with him, she had allowed some glimpses into her mind. But wanting a thing and knowing what was right for her was not the same. She had to give the little girl the same life as she'd had if she were going to survive. Or as close to it as she could manage under the circumstances, strange as they were.

"No. You leave her alone."

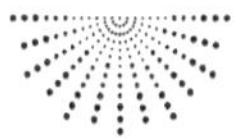

*W*eston was gone.

The room was quiet. They could hear sounds outside of it; music, shouting, the sound of traffic; but inside it was quiet as they all looked at each other.

"Is that it?" Reg asked. "That isn't it." She didn't need Harrison to answer. She already knew. Weston may have given up on that particular battle, but he would be back. None of them could know whether it would be an hour, a day, or a millennium, but sooner or later, he would be back causing more trouble than ever. Reg just hoped that they would have a break. After the stand-off, she really needed a good nap.

Reg looked at Corvin and realized she was still drawing on his powers. She hurriedly broke from him, and he staggered in place for an instant, his face a waxen gray.

"Sorry. Are you okay?"

"For someone who has been so vehement about me stealing powers, you are remarkably quick to use mine."

"Uh…" Reg wasn't sure what to say. "I wasn't… I didn't even think about that."

"At least *I* get permission."

"Well, sort of," she pointed out, "some of the time. It isn't like you can claim to have been that diligent about it. At least, not with me. I guess… I just didn't think about it. I thought that since you came, you were on-board with what we were doing."

"I didn't exactly come of my own free choice."

Reg looked at Harrison. "Did you bring him against his will?"

Harrison made a brushing-away gesture with his hand. "Humans have such weak wills; it is hard to say."

"Harrison. Really. Did you bring him here without asking?"

"I told you what I was doing."

"But… that's not the same as asking."

"I think it's close enough," he assured her.

Reg gave one bark of laughter and shook her head. She looked back at Corvin. "Immortals! I'm sorry. Will you be okay?"

"I just need a few minutes of recovery time. I'm not used to expending energy so quickly."

"Yeah. Okay. Next time I'll try to remember to ask."

"I'm hoping there won't be a next time." Corvin wiped a dab of shaving cream off of his ear.

Reg turned her attention to the others. Norma Jean was staring at her, eyes glassy with shock. She had been happy when Weston had been flirting with her and paying her compliments, but the battle and Weston's vanishing act had been too weird for her.

She had that look that Reg had seen in the eyes of others when they couldn't believe what they had seen Reg do. Withdrawal, a blank aspect, and then, eventually, revision of those memories, rewriting them into something that made sense. Probably some version of Reg playing a prank on them.

Reg felt a kinship with Loki, the Norse god who was always referred to as a trickster. She hated being painted as the naughty girl who was always trying to trick people and pull something over on the adults who were her caregivers.

Then Reg looked at herself. The little girl who would grow up to be her, or some version of her. Being so young, she would be a lot more resilient than Norma Jean. She would probably believe what she had seen for years to come, until she was old enough to realize that it was impossible and must have just been something that she had come up with in her overactive imagination.

"Are you okay?" Reg asked.

The little girl nodded. Reg wet a thumb and rubbed away a smudge of dirt on the girl's pale cheek. She tried to clean away another and found that it was not dirt, but a bruise. Reg stroked her hair instead, smoothing down the tangled red locks and hoping to soothe away the trauma of what she had just experienced.

"Everything is going to be okay. I don't think he'll come back here again. And Uncle Harrison will keep an eye on you. Won't you, Harrison?"

Harrison nodded cheerfully. He was holding Starlight and petting him. Reg frowned. She didn't think he'd been holding the cat a moment before. Had he disappeared, transporting back to Francesca's house in the future, and then back again, all in the blink of an eye? Or had Starlight once lived there, right in little Reg's own building, and she had never known it? It was all too confusing for Reg to sort out.

The little girl's eyes sparkled when she saw the cat. "Oh, a kitty! Can I pat your kitty?"

She wriggled to get away from Reg. Reg put her down gently, and she hurried over to Harrison. Harrison obligingly stooped down to let her pet Starlight, and when the little girl showed that she could be gentle and pet him nicely, he sat down on the dirty carpet and released Starlight, letting him explore the room and wind his way around the little girl's legs. She was in transports of delight, petting the cat and talking to him like a baby, then growing more serious and talking to him as if he were having an actual conversation with her.

Reg noticed that Starlight didn't beg for food like he normally would have; maybe he knew that even if there were a few crumbs of food in the apartment, there wasn't anything to spare for him.

"Look, Mommy!" The little girl tried to get her mother's attention. "Look, Unca Harrison broughted a kitty! Can I keep him? He's so nice!"

Norma Jean focused on the cat and shook her head. "You know you can't have a cat, Regina. How many times do I have to tell you?"

"But this one is so nice. I take care'f him. He would catch mice!"

"I said no, Reg! Don't argue with Mommy!"

The little girl shrank back and fell silent. She sat on the floor, petting Starlight when he rubbed against her and pulling him into her lap to cuddle him. Her face was sad and resigned.

Reg watched the cat and the little girl interact. Maybe that was how she and Starlight had recognized each other when Reg had gone to the shelter looking for a cat.

Except that wasn't the way that things had happened in Reg's past. Not in her timeline. But it would be in the revised thread of time.

She shook her head, deciding not to try to understand it.

* * *

Harrison must have had a little more understanding of humans than he pretended. He didn't return everyone to Francesca's house, but Reg found herself in her own cottage with just Starlight and Harrison. She bent down and picked Starlight up, holding his warm, soft fur against her face and trying to see Harrison's blurred form through teary eyes.

"Will she be okay?" she asked.

Harrison's laugh rumbled deep in his chest. "You're here," he pointed out. "And you got your tuxedo cat and cottage near the ocean."

It took a few moments for Reg to realize that the little girl had grown up to be her, and wasn't a scared, lonely child anymore. What had happened decades ago was part of the misty past, something she could barely remember anymore.

"That's… just weird."

Harrison smiled. "I think you turned out okay, Regina."

"So nothing changed? It all happened the way I remember?"

"That depends what you remember."

"Harrison…" Reg rubbed at the pain in her forehead. Too much psychic work in one day. The spot that Sarah referred to as her third eye was pulsing with pain and no matter whether it was day or night, she was going to climb into bed, pull the covers over her eyes, and sleep for at least eight hours.

"Go sleep it off," he agreed, reaching out to take Starlight from her arms. "Temporal travel is always hard on human bodies. At least you didn't throw up."

"Weston is gone, right? He's not going to be back tomorrow trying to take over the world?"

"He's not gone. But he knows there are opposing forces and he won't be too quick to interfere in humans' affairs again. It's easier to seek satisfaction on other planes."

"And you don't have to worry about those things? What do you do if there are no humans to oppose him? Why couldn't you be the one to challenge him?"

"It is against the rules for me to harm one of my own kind."

"But Corvin and I didn't harm him. Why couldn't you do what we could?"

"It's not my world." Harrison shrugged. He twisted the ends of his mustache. "You will sleep well."

As usual, she didn't know whether it was a command or a prediction. And she didn't care.

"You going to come in, Star?"

Starlight made a soft purr-meow and Reg nodded. "Okay. See you in a bit."

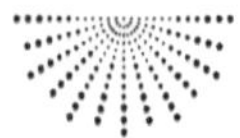

There was a knock at her door. Reg sipped her tea, then got up to see who it was. She wasn't expecting any appointments until after dark.

She couldn't see anyone through the peephole and, after hesitating for a moment, opened the door anyway to see if UPS had left a package on the doorstep. Forst and Fir stood there together, below the level of the peephole. Reg smiled, genuinely happy to see them.

"Hi! I didn't know you were coming. How is everything?" She wasn't sure whether she should invite them in for tea. Inviting pixies in was a bad thing, but what about gnomes? She didn't think they would do anything mischievous.

"We brought you a living thing," Fir said, displaying a small green plant in a pot. He held it reverently with both hands and looked down at it with a smile. "Every home should have a living."

Reg held her hands out to receive it from him. "I do have Starlight, he's a living thing, but you're right; I don't have a plant."

"They help to keep the air clean and make you happy."

Both gnomes smiled at her, showing that they were happy. Their cheeks were round and rosy in spite of the many wrinkles from working in the sun.

"Thank you so much." Reg studied the plant. "It isn't the endangered one, is it? They wouldn't let you dig up the, uh, cluster…"

"Clustervine. No. It is not the clustervine. That is still safe on my plot, thanks to Reg Rawlins."

Reg smiled. "Good. And where should I put this little fellow? Does he like to be right by the window?"

"North facing. Diffuse light." Fir poked his head in Reg's door to look around. He pointed to one of the side tables in Reg's living room area. "It would like that space."

"I'll put it there, then. I've never had a plant before, so I don't know if I have a green thumb. How much water do I give it?"

"Once every week or two, enough to keep the dirt moist when you push your finger into it. Not enough to drown it."

"Okay. I hope I can manage that." She knew how much they loved plants and how much it would hurt Fir if he knew she neglected his gift. Maybe Sarah would help her to keep an eye on it too, just to make sure she didn't forget about it for a month at a time.

"And don't let the cat eat it," Forst warned. "Sometimes, cats eat things they shouldn't."

Fir nodded solemnly.

* * *

Reg hadn't wanted to go to Davyn's office again, but she was also not prepared to invite him to her house. Even though she was getting better at building a wall of protection around herself, she was by no means an expert. Corvin had still been able to trick her into giving him admission and she hadn't had the strength to fight back. That stung, and she didn't want to provide Davyn with an opportunity for an attack either. He was the leader of his coven and, while Reg didn't know all of what that entailed, she figured that meant that he was a pretty powerful warlock, despite appearances. Just because he hadn't done anything to threaten her in previous meetings, that didn't mean she could trust him. He was a close friend of Corvin's and didn't seem to understand the way the modern world worked.

So, she had only agreed to meet with him again if they did so in a public place, and it could not be The Crystal Bowl or anywhere she might run into someone she knew. Davyn suggested the dining room in a nearby hotel. They could have a meal, they'd be around other people, but not likely anyone she knew. It would mostly be frequented by out-of-town guests, which would be ideal for their purposes.

That had been her reasoning, anyway.

"The Council has made a decision not to readmit Corvin to the coven quite yet," Davyn informed Reg when their meals came and they had exhausted the usual small talk. "I wanted to let you know this personally and to reassure you that we are not just taking his word that he has mended his ways. We will continue to watch him and to evaluate his actions to decide whether he can be... a safe and productive member of our society."

Reg pushed food around on her plate. She had been hungry, and the delicious smells of the chicken stir fry had smelled good when the waiter put it down in front of her, but talking about Corvin and his behavior or his potential return to full member-ship of the coven made her forget how hungry she had been.

"Well, that's good," she said slowly. "I'm glad you weren't fooled by him."

"It has come to our attention, however, that you have been seen with him again in... possibly compromising circumstances. I am concerned about these reports."

"Why?"

"It is my duty to be aware of what Corvin is doing in the community... something like a probation officer. And his continued relationship with you is concerning. I'm also a little confused about why you are seeing him socially when you are so adamant about him not being returned to our society. It seemed like a conflict."

Reg searched for a coherent argument. She didn't really have any excuse for agreeing to see Corvin after all the conflict they had experienced already. Her choice had, once again, resulted in her being put in a dangerous situation with him. Saying that she had been testing him to see if he would resist his impulses seemed like the best story, but it didn't exactly put her in a good light. If she was afraid of Corvin and objected to what he had done in the past, then why put herself in that position again, even as a test?

She pushed a piece of chicken around and eventually put it into her mouth and chewed slowly. Davyn waited for her response.

"I just… I don't know. He wears me down. He uses his charms, and I forget how dangerous he is… I just want to be able to do what I want and still be safe."

She took a sip of her wine.

"I guess I want to believe that he has reformed or that I am strong enough to resist him. But instead… each time the results are the same. We start the evening with my rules firmly in place… but by the end of it, he has the upper hand again, and all my arguments and protests and the barriers that I have tried to build up are gone."

"It's a dangerous game. Why don't you simply avoid him?"

"I try. But he says that we're bonded together. Whatever decisions I make… our futures are still intertwined."

Davyn looked troubled by this. He nodded slowly and took a few bites of his dinner. They sat in silence, each considering the matter.

"Do you think that if you moved, he would follow you?"

"Why should I have to move?" Reg snapped.

"You don't. I'm asking you what you think would happen. You're a fortune teller, aren't you? Why don't you give me a prediction of the future? If you chose to move, would he follow you? Or would that break the connection between you?"

Reg sighed. She thought about it. What if she decided it was time to move on? Not back north, but maybe across the country to California or Nevada. If she put enough miles between them, that would be the end of it, wouldn't it? That would be the end of the conflict and any potential relationship with Corvin.

A vision started to fill her mind. She felt a strong hand in hers, imagined his breath in her ear and his husky voice coming to her in the night. But it wasn't Corvin. How could it be? She could never have a romantic relationship with him without risking the loss of her powers. She could only have that kind of relationship with a warlock who couldn't take her powers. An equal like Davyn or—

Reg swore and looked around. She knew exactly who could put a vision like that into her head. And once she was looking for him, she spotted Damon across the room, watching her, his face flushed with jealousy.

Davyn turned, following her gaze. "An admirer?" he asked lightly.

Reg shook her head. "This is getting ridiculous. I can have dinner with anyone I like!"

"Of course you can," Davyn agreed. "If he can't understand that, maybe you should tell him to leave you alone."

Which was precisely what Reg had done. But he was back, still trying to fill her head with his visions, twisting what she wanted to suit himself.

"Where is a magical restraining order when you need it?"

Under the weight of both of their gazes, Damon eventually caved and walked out of the room. Reg didn't see him again when she left.

She was sure it was only a coincidence that he had seen her there. He was acting as a security guard at some conference being held at the hotel. He had said so the other day.

It had just been a coincidence that he had seen her there with Davyn.

* * *

Reg had agreed to go with Francesca as she shipped Sally and Horace to their new owners in China and Egypt. Each carried one crate with an unhappy black kattakyn inside, leaving the house with Nicole's mournful cries ringing in their ears. It was heartbreaking to have to separate them, but they both knew it was necessary to keep the Witch Doctor from re-forming any time in the near future. And Francesca could not keep ten cats, even if they hadn't been the Witch Doctor's draugrs.

"Do you think the kittens knew about Weston being detained in your house?" Reg asked, hoping to distract them both from the unhappy felines. She was a little irritated with Francesca for hiding in the kitchen when Reg had accidentally released Weston. But then again, Francesca had experience with one immortal and Reg could understand her not wanting to get involved with another. "Is that why they went to the basement? If they are still the Witch Doctor at some level, they must have sensed that their old rival was there."

"I do not know," Francesca admitted. "It was very strange to have them disappearing in the house, when there was no way to get into the attic or the basement. There was strange magic going on in the house."

"Maybe it was the wormhole. Maybe that's how they kept getting into inaccessible rooms."

Francesca nodded in agreement. "Probably."

"They haven't disappeared again since then?"

She shook her head, lips pressed together. "No. But I also performed some cleansing rituals… did you notice the house seems brighter and more cheerful now? I think that immortal of yours must have been what was causing it to be so gloomy."

"He's not *my* immortal."

If one of the immortals was hers, it was Harrison. He was the one who had tried to protect her and had been there through the hard times. Then again, Weston was her father, and he *had* tried to go back to change the course of Reg's life, but neither of them was really *her* immortal. They had their own minds and wills.

"Well, anyway, I'm glad your house is feeling better now. I guess you'll be happy when it's just you and Nicole again and things have settled down."

"Yes, of course." Francesca sighed. "It will seem very empty with only one cat."

"Maybe you could get a plant too. I hear they are good company."

Francesca looked at her with pursed lips, puzzled by her comment. She shrugged. "Perhaps."

"It's a big house. You could get more than one plant."

Francesca didn't offer any response to this. They carried the cat crates into the small airport. Reg expected to just check them in with the luggage and leave them there, but after registering with the private airline counter, they were instructed to wait with the crates until the pilot was ready to take possession of them.

When the pilot showed up, Reg was surprised to see a young man she already knew. She hurried forward to shake his hand. "Warren Blake! How are you doing?"

His face was much fuller than the last time she had seen him, quite gaunt from being in a magical coma in a nursing home. He looked much more alive and happy than he had before.

"Reg Rawlins!" He pumped her hand, brown eyes alight. "We should have you over to dinner one day! Ling would love to see you."

"Yes, we should get together," Reg agreed. It was nice to see him looking so well and happy after all that he had been through. "I guess you're flying our cats today."

"To the international airport in Miami," Warren agreed. "Not all the way to their destinations." He looked into the crates and wiggled his finger through the bars to engage with the cats. They just huddled there, looking miserable. Warren checked the big stickers on each of the crates with their destination information. "Wow. World travelers. Well, don't you worry, I'll get them safely to Miami, and the airline is very good with these special deliveries."

Francesca was teary-eyed but seemed happy that Horace and Sally were going with someone Reg knew and trusted. Reg didn't tell him that the last time she had dealt with Warren, it had been after a plane crash. What were the chances that Warren would have a second crash? He was probably the safest pilot they could choose. He couldn't be unlucky enough to crash a second time.

They both said their teary goodbyes to the kittens and left them with Warren.

* * *

Reg's phone started ringing as she got to the door of her cottage. She fumbled with her key and hurried to put down her grocery bags and dig out the phone, not wanting to answer it on the doorstep.

It was an unknown number—a Maine area code. Reg hesitated before answering. Had someone from her old life tracked her down?

It wouldn't be the police. They wouldn't bother to call her. They'd contact the police department and work with them to get Reg into custody. And it had been a long time since she had operated in Maine, anyway. No one there would still be looking for her.

It was probably just a telemarketer. If they could operate out of India, then why not out of Maine? She swiped the screen to answer and brought the phone up to her ear.

"Hello?"

"Is this Reg Rawlins?" The voice, its tone, accent, and cadence were startlingly familiar. Reg shook off the feeling of deja vu, frowning.

"Who is this?"

"You probably don't remember me, but I knew you a long time ago when you were just a little girl." There was a hitch, a hesitation. "My name is Norma Jean."

Reg kept the phone at her ear, her mind spinning. Her legs

folded under her and she sat down in the middle of the kitchen floor.

"Norma Jean?" she whispered. Norma Jean was alive. But hadn't she been killed by the Witch Doctor?

Not, it dawned on her slowly, in the new timeline. She and Corvin had banished the Witch Doctor. Weston had returned to his lover and child in the past where they were well and safe. Reg and Corvin had been able to persuade him to leave, but in a timeline where there was no Witch Doctor in corporeal form to hurt Norma Jean.

"They took you away from me when you were just a little mite," Norma Jean explained. "They said I couldn't take proper care of you and they put you into foster care. I didn't get clean for a long time after that, and when I did, they said my rights had been terminated. I couldn't get you back."

Reg swallowed, not sure what to say.

"I've been looking for you for a long time, honey," Norma Jean went on. "I'd like to come and see you."

Did you enjoy this book? Reviews and recommendations are vital to making a book successful.

Please leave a review at your favorite book store or review site and share it with your friends.

Don't miss the following bonus material:
Sign up for mailing list to get a free ebook
Read a sneak preview chapter
Other books by P.D. Workman
Learn more about the author

Sign up for my mailing list at pdworkman.com and get Gluten-Free Murder for free!

PREVIEW OF DELUSIONS OF THE PAST

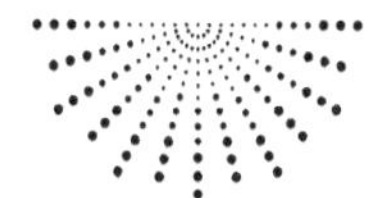

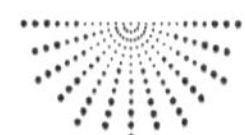

Reg didn't recognize her right away. She looked at the woman who stood on the doorstep of the cottage and raised her eyebrows questioningly, wondering who she was and what she was there for. She didn't have a lanyard with ID to identify her as a canvasser for any charity or a utility repair person. She wasn't someone that Reg recognized from the area. She might be a client that Sarah, Reg's landlord, had lined up or someone who had seen Reg's advertising and decided to drop by instead of making an appointment as requested in all of her posters.

Reg cocked her head and was about to ask the woman who she was when she suddenly realized. The woman looked a lot different now. Clean and tidy, her shoulder-length brunette hair smooth and silky, her face enhanced by a little makeup and not covered with sores and pockmarks. She'd had her teeth done. Maybe a full set of dentures or implants. She bore little resemblance to the mother that Reg remembered.

"Norma Jean," Reg said, heart sinking.

Norma Jean smiled brilliantly, showing off the perfect teeth. "Oh, my baby. It's been so long since I saw you!"

She fell upon Reg, embracing her, trying to pull her in close for one of those warm Hallmark moments. Reg pulled back, pushing her away, trying to get her personal space back. "Don't do that! Don't touch me."

Norma Jean's eyebrows went up, and the corners of her mouth went down. She gave Reg a kicked-puppy-dog look, all hurt and offended.

Reg held her hands up in front of her in a 'stop' signal. "You can't just go around hugging people. You're not my mother. Not anymore."

"I am your mother and will never stop being your mother, no matter what you say or do." The slight southern cadence and accent were the same as Reg remembered. That woman had lived in her head for decades, from the time she had died when Reg was four, until… Reg shook her head to try to rid it of the feeling of vertigo she felt whenever considering the timeline and the changes that Weston had caused when he went back to see her mother.

Norma Jean had died when Reg was four. But not in the timeline Reg now inhabited. Whatever Weston had done had changed essential parts of Reg's past. Norma Jean had not died. Her spirit had not attached itself to Reg, her guilt making her a constant companion, always telling Reg what to do and attempting to undo the harm she had done while she had been alive.

Reg just stared at Norma Jean, trying to comprehend it all.

"Well, aren't you going to invite me in?" Norma Jean queried, giving a flirty little pout, acting the role she had made up. Why had she suddenly shown up in Black Sands, Florida? Reg had made it clear that she didn't want to see Norma Jean. Either Norma Jean was thicker than Reg believed, or she had wholly disregarded what her daughter had said, deciding to fly in from Maine regardless.

"Fine, come in," Reg said finally, glancing around the yard to make sure Norma Jean was the only one there. She wasn't sure who else she was looking for. Weston or a more current boyfriend? There was no way for her to prevent the powerful immortal from entering even if she tried.

She opened the door wide enough for Norma Jean and stepped back.

Norma Jean gave a smile and came in, acting like the queen of Black Sands. She looked around Reg's little cottage, chin lifted, smile set firmly in place. Reg went to the kitchen to put on a kettle for tea, an action that had become habitual since she had moved to Black Sands and started seeing clients for psychic readings. A cup of tea always went over well with someone who was about to take a foray into the unknown. And Reg could read the tea leaves in the bottom of the cup if they were so inclined. Reg would go with whatever psychic reading method they preferred.

"This is real nice," Norma Jean told her.

"Yeah." Reg wasn't in much of a mood for conversation. It was just a cottage in the back yard of Sarah's big house, but it was better than anything else Reg had ever had on her own. Clean and neat and furnished in Sarah's breezy Florida style. Certainly better than anything that Reg had ever lived in while she was still with Norma Jean, a series of flophouses, shelters, and cold nights on the street.

She watched the kettle intently, hoping that it would take all day to boil.

Norma Jean wandered around, looking at the decorations and furnishings. She touched the leaves of the plant that Fir had given to Reg when he told her that she needed living things in her environment. It did perk the place up a bit, giving the cottage a more homey feeling. Fir said that plants had feelings, and maybe Reg was sensing the warm feelings of the houseplant itself. Or perhaps it just looked good on the little side table.

Eventually, Norma Jean settled on the wicker couch and waited for Reg to make the tea and bring it over on the tray. She helped herself to one of the cups, and they both gave their attention to their tea, Reg studiously ignoring Norma Jean, until it was no longer possible, because Norma Jean was talking, forcing Reg to acknowledge her existence.

"They took you away from me when you were still real little."

She took a tentative sip of the tea but didn't look like she enjoyed it. Reg couldn't remember Norma Jean ever drinking tea. She would probably have preferred the Jack Daniels in Reg's corner cupboard. "I didn't have any say in it. I would have kept you if I could."

Norma Jean had been destitute and addicted, completely unable to care for a child. The times that she had ignored Reg had been the best. Better to be ignored than abused. It was a wonder that it had taken child services four years to apprehend her.

"You couldn't be a mother."

"No... I guess I couldn't," Norma Jean admitted. "I needed to take care of myself and deal with my own problems before I could be responsible for someone else."

Taking care of herself was all Norm Jean had ever done, self-serving and focused on her own gratification. How long had it taken for her to get straight after Reg had been removed? Ten years? Twenty?

Reg played with one of the red box-braids that hung down next to her face. It had taken Norma Jean twenty-five years to make contact with her daughter again. How much of that time had she been clean and sober?

"I'm sorry that you had to grow up in foster care. I would have gotten you back if I could have. But they wouldn't even talk about letting you come back unless I cleaned up my act. And..." Norma Jean wavered, "after I was off the drugs, I decided it was probably best if you stayed there. I needed to figure things out... learn how to support myself. I recognized that I didn't have what I needed to take care of a kid."

"Good for you."

"I've been looking for you. Once you were old enough to look after yourself, I kind of looked around... tried to find out where you might be... but I couldn't find you. They wouldn't give me any information, of course; those government agencies act like they're so superior and won't tell you a thing. I thought... that maybe you might be looking for me too. Once you aged out of the system, then you could go wherever you wanted to and you could look for me."

Reg shook her head. Of course she had never searched for Norma Jean. She had known exactly where Norma Jean was. Dead and lurking in a corner of Reg's brain. She had tried to banish the voice, not to go back there. Her life with Norma Jean had never been a happy place. She hadn't liked the instability of foster care, but she had rarely wished she was back with Norma Jean again. "They told me you were dead," she told Norma Jean flatly.

"What? Why would they do that? They knew I wasn't dead!"

"Well, that's what I thought."

Norma Jean shook her head angrily. "I should sue them! I cannot believe that they would lie to you like that. We could have been reunited years ago."

Reg sipped her tea, not answering. She wouldn't have wanted to have reunited with Norma Jean.

Or would she? In the timeline where Norma Jean had not been killed, had Reg yearned to be back together with her again? If she'd known that Norma Jean was alive, would Reg have gone back to her once she was sixteen or eighteen and had a mind of her own? At least there would have been someone in her life who was a constant, even if Norma Jean wasn't able to provide the care of a parent. It would have been better than being out on the streets, as Reg had been several times since her graduation from foster care.

There was a soft thud, and Reg turned her head to watch Starlight come out of the bedroom to see who was visiting.

* * *

Norma Jean looked at the tuxedo cat with the mismatched eyes and white spot on his forehead, her eyebrows drawing down in puzzlement. Starlight went to Reg's side and, after surveying Norma Jean for a moment, jumped up into Reg's lap. Reg put down her tea and petted him, stroking the longer fur down his back and scratching his ears and chin. Norma Jean shook her head.

"Where have I seen that cat before?"

Reg knew very well where she had seen the cat, but thought it interesting that Starlight would seem more familiar to Norma Jean than her own daughter. Did she not remember the woman who had been with the cat? Or had her drug-addled brain lost that detail or morphed it into something else?

"Maybe you saw a cat that looked like him," Reg said. "This is Starlight."

"You always wanted a cat. I don't know how many times you dragged some stray in and tried to convince me that you would take care of it."

"Did I?" Reg didn't remember that. But she didn't remember a lot of specific experiences from when she'd been with Norma Jean. She had, after all, only been four. A lot of people didn't remember anything before they were five, not just traumatized kids taken into custody after a parent was murdered. Maybe Norma Jean remembered only that one time when little Reg had met Starlight and hugged and cuddled him and asked if she could keep him. Maybe that had become 'dragging home random strays and asking to keep them.' Parents did that sometimes. Blew one little incident up into something the child 'always' did.

Reg put her face against the top of Starlight's head and breathed into his fur. It was always very calming to hold Starlight. He gave out good vibes. He had chosen Reg when she went to the animal shelter, rather than her choosing him, and she was glad that he had.

"So, tell me all about your life." Norma Jean leaned forward. "I want to know everything. When you were little, where you've been, and what you've done. If you have a boyfriend. What you're doing all the way in Black Sands."

Reg disliked sharing information about her past. She particularly didn't want to give Norma Jean any ammunition. Who knew how she might use it.

"Nothing to tell. This is just where I moved. Now I try to make a living… doing personal consulting."

"Personal consulting," Norma Jean tasted the words. "What exactly is that? What kind of consulting?"

"Life planning. Making decisions about the future. I help people to… look ahead in their lives. Or sometimes, to take a look back at the past and make their peace so that they can move forward again."

"That sounds very interesting." Norma Jean was impressed. "How do you get all of your business? You must make good money to live in a place like this."

Reg cleared her throat. "It isn't as much as you might think. My landlord helps me get some work; she's really… tuned into the community. I advertise, mostly locally, put posters up on community bulletin boards or places they might frequent. It's picking up steadily."

She always worried about how long it would last, and wished that she'd discovered a treasure like gold or jewels instead of Weston. Why couldn't it have been gold?

"Maybe you could help me. I'm always so confused about where to go with my life… I guess I don't have very much direction. I don't have any big talents. You must have gotten an education, to be able to do that kind of life planning for people."

"All self-educated. I didn't have any money to go to college. Nowhere to live. No one to cosign a loan. I didn't do great in school, so there were no grants or scholarships."

"Yeah. That's the trouble with foster care. I've heard it's really hard."

She'd heard it. Too bad she hadn't lived it. She might not be so sanguine about it.

"What about you? What are *you* doing?" Reg turned the question back on Norma Jean. She had enough money to buy a plane ticket across the country. She looked well-fed and focused. Not gaunt and wretched and scattered, unable to conceive of how to make it from one day to the next.

"I do a little of this and a little of that… just whatever I can pick up. That's why I said I should have you give me one of those consultations."

"You pick up what kind of work? Cleaning? Cooking? Outdoor work? Hooking?"

Norma gave a shocked laugh. "Oh, not that! Yes, sometimes cleaning or outdoor stuff like mowing lawns. Some retail stores. Just… positions that don't require any experience. I don't have much on my resume. Employers don't think much of that."

The same kind of jobs as Reg had hopscotched between until she had happened onto the psychic gig. That had worked well enough that she'd been able to give up the back-breaking, footsore work.

Reg got to her feet and put Starlight down. She moved around restlessly. She didn't like having Norma Jean there. It made her anxious. She was too anxious and restless to sit in one place and chat as if they were old friends.

She went to the window and looked out into the yard. The grass was all neatly trimmed around the paving stones that made up the pathway. She couldn't see the main garden from that side of the cottage, but she could see well-maintained bushes, trees, and lawn. It had looked nice before, and since Sarah had hired Forst as a gardener, everything was looking lush and bright and happy. He had done an excellent job.

A movement in the corner of her eye caught Reg's attention, and she turned her head to look at it, but as soon as she did so, it was gone. She watched for a moment to see if it came back. Maybe a bird or the wind blowing a tree. She waited for the movement to repeat itself but she didn't see it again.

"What are you looking at?" Norma Jean inquired.

"Nothing. I'm just looking." Reg moved away from the window again. "So, how long are you here? What are your plans? I use the second bedroom as my office, so there is nowhere here for you to stay overnight."

"Oh, I would never impose on you," Norma Jean assured, her

voice earnest and smooth. Reg didn't believe it for a minute. Norma Jean had been hoping for an invitation, or failing receipt of an invitation, to be able to talk her way into staying in Reg's cottage while she was in town. Reg hoped that she couldn't find anywhere to sleep and had to go back home right away.

Reg drifted into the kitchen and cleared a few dirty dishes away. Norma Jean watched and didn't offer to help. Not that there were enough dishes for her to help with. By the time she got to the kitchen, Reg would have been done.

There was a quick tap at the door, then the handle turned and Sarah bustled in. "Good morning, Reg. Isn't it a lovely day out there today? Oh." Her eyes settled on Norma Jean. "I didn't know that you had company."

Reg didn't have quite what it took to say 'she was just leaving' to get Norma Jean out of the way. "This is… Norma Jean." Reg swallowed and tried to think of how much information to share. "My mother."

Sarah looked stunned. She put a hand over her heart. "Your mother? But I thought your mother—"

Reg waited for Sarah to say "was dead," but she trailed off, not finishing the thought.

"Apparently not. That's what they told me, back when I was little, but I guess it was just a lie."

"Well, this is quite a shock." Sarah landed heavily in the chair that Reg had recently vacated. "That's amazing news. How… wonderful for you." Sarah smiled at Norma Jean, turned her head and looked at Reg, and the smile on her face faltered.

"I was so excited to be able to track Reg down," Norma Jean gushed. "And you must be her friend…?"

"Sarah." Sarah stuck out her hand to Norma Jean and shook vigorously. "Yes, I'm Reg's friend and her landlord."

"Oh, so this is your place."

Sarah nodded. "Well, I own it, but it's Reg's for as long as she wants to live here. I needed someone stable to take it for me. Reg has been a lifesaver for me."

Did Norma Jean know she was being lied to? Reg didn't do anything for Sarah but pay a minimal rent for the cottage. Sarah came and went, keeping everything clean and tidy, feeding Starlight when he insisted he was hungry, lining up clients for Reg, delivering her mail and flyers, and telling her about the community events coming up. She was like… a mother to Reg.

Maybe Norma Jean sensed this. Her mouth was a straight line, lips pressed together. She didn't like this interloper in Reg's life.

But to Reg, Norma Jean was the interloper. Who did she think she was, showing up on Reg's doorstep without any warning and expecting to be invited in and even being allowed to stay with her for… however long Norma Jean was planning to stay? Reg bit her lip, worrying about that. Norma Jean hadn't said anything to indicate that she had ties back home. She might be planning to move to Black Sands permanently. A choice that would make things very difficult for Reg.

"It's very nice to meet you," Sarah told Norma Jean pleasantly. "I'm sure Reg will have the best time while you are here."

Norma Jean gave a broad smile, which to Reg looked utterly fake. She nodded vigorously. "Oh, yes, we are going to have the best time, aren't we honey?"

Reg didn't try to match Norma Jean's smile. The answer was no; they were not going to have the best time. Reg looked around, trying to figure out some way of getting out of the situation. She looked back at Sarah, wondering whether she could see the panic in Reg's eyes.

"Did you… need something, Sarah?"

"Well…"

"Did you need me to do something for you? Norma Jean can go, I'm free if there's something that you wanted…"

"No, no. It's not that. It's just that I needed to do some maintenance here. I know I haven't given you the proper forty-eight hours' notice, so I really shouldn't spring it on you like this, but I was going to see whether you were going to… be out for part of the day. and then if you are, I could come back then to work on it."

"Oh." Reg looked around. "Well, you gotta do what you gotta do. Norma Jean, we're going to have to vacate, so…"

"Are you going to go out to lunch?" Sarah suggested. "You could take her to The Crystal Bowl. Maybe go out shopping for a while or go for a walk in the park. Then by the time you are done, I'm sure I'd be mostly finished here."

"Oh, yes, let's!" Norma Jean jumped in. "That sounds like fun."

Reg glared at Sarah. "I don't think that I can fit that into my schedule today."

"You can make time for your mother who you haven't seen in years," Norma Jean pouted. "It's my treat. I don't know the restaurants in the area, so you'll have to tell me what's good, but I'll take you out and we'll have a nice time."

"Go," Sarah encouraged, making a motion to shoo Reg out of the room. "You go on. Have a good time. I need the space to work."

Reg shook her head. "What about Starlight?" she grumbled. "Do you need me to lock him up? What are you going to be working on?"

Sarah looked at the cat. She was not a cat person and would probably prefer that he weren't underfoot, but she was always good about it and didn't make a fuss. "Oh, no. He'll be fine. I'll only have the door open for a few minutes, and I'll keep an eye on him to make sure he can't get out."

"And he won't be in your way? You know how he has to get right in the middle of whatever you're working on."

"He won't bother me. The two of you go ahead, go have a nice lunch together."

Reg fetched her purse, moving slowly, still trying to think of an excuse to get out of it. She could tell Norma Jean that she had somewhere else to go. A competing appointment. But Norma Jean was going to know that something was up. And she would keep persisting until she got her own way. At least if they were going to lunch together, there was a natural break point where they could each say their goodbyes and go their separate directions. She only had to put up with Norma Jean for an hour or two.

That sounded like a very long time.

CHAPTER TWO

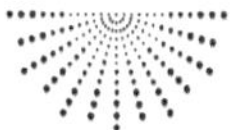

When Reg got back from lunch, it was quite late. She had intentionally given Sarah a couple of extra hours to finish whatever she was working on at the cottage. Norma Jean had pouted and whined about Reg having to take care of other matters, but she couldn't have expected to have all of Reg's time. Reg was running a business. Norma Jean had grudgingly accepted this, and though she had tried to get Reg to let her stay at the cottage, Reg had been firm about that. She didn't have a second bed and Norma Jean wasn't sharing Reg's.

"When are you going back north? There isn't really anything for you to do here."

"What do you mean, there isn't anything for me to do? I am here to see my daughter. I want to know all about you. Really get to know you. We've lost so many years."

"Norma Jean…" Reg held up her hand in protest. "I told you not to come here. I think I've been pretty nice to let you into my house and to go out to lunch with you, but you have to understand, you're not a part of my life. And you're not going to be."

"You can't *not* be my daughter. I gave birth to you and nothing is going to change that."

Reg wasn't sure that either of those statements was true. The more she discovered about the magical world, the less confident she was of anything. Maybe Norma Jean had given birth to her in the usual way, or maybe Weston, being an immortal, had somehow created Reg in a different way. And just because something had always been one way, that didn't mean that it couldn't change. Norma Jean had been dead for almost Reg's whole life, and now she wasn't. If that could change, anything could.

There were lights when she approached the cottage. Reg was surprised that Sarah would have left them on. She should have finished earlier in the day when it was not dark, and wouldn't have thought to leave the lights on for her. Reg hung back from the cottage, looking things over, hesitating about what she should do.

She was being silly. What did she think? That there was someone else in her cottage? That someone had broken in? Or that Norma Jean had arrived back ahead of her, refusing to listen to Reg's refusal to let her stay for the night? If Norma Jean was there, Reg was going to call the police. She'd had enough of her mother's nonsense and wanted to make it clear that she was not welcome there. She could go back north and do whatever she wanted to, as long as it was far away from Reg.

A shadow passed across the window. Not Starlight. Definitely a person.

Reg heard the faint tinkle of bells, which didn't seem like they came from inside the house. Maybe a neighbor had recently installed new wind chimes. Reg couldn't remember hearing them before then.

Was it Norma Jean? Or another intruder? Should she call the police? She didn't want to have any more dealings with the police in Black Sands and didn't need to attract any attention to herself.

Reg crept up to the window and tried to peek inside without exposing herself. If it was just Norma Jean, there was nothing to be afraid of. But if it was some other person or shadowy creature, she wasn't about to go barging in and get herself eaten or cursed.

She watched for the intruder, waiting for them to cross back across the window again. She was at a bad angle and couldn't see inside very well. She could go around to a window with a better view of the interior, but then she would have to contend with the horizontal blinds.

The intruder came closer to the window and, straining her neck for a better angle, Reg finally relaxed. It was just Sarah. Still there after so long? The maintenance must not have gone the way she had hoped.

Reg went to the door and hesitated, wondering if she should knock before entering so that she wouldn't startle Sarah. But knocking on her own door? That didn't seem right. Reg opened the door, jingling her keys, and went in.

She stopped, stock still, her mouth open, as she looked around at the changes to the cottage.

* * *

"Holy cow! What happened here?"

Sarah beamed at Reg. "Do you like it?"

Reg didn't know where to look first. There was what she was pretty sure was holly, with shiny green leaves and red berries, and another plant with white berries. There were strings of twinkle lights and a wide assortment of candles flickering in jars around the room. There was an evergreen tree in a bucket and wreaths, pinecones, and garlands everywhere. It seemed like every surface was covered with some new decoration.

"Is this for Christmas? It looks like a department store blew up in here!"

"For Yule," Sarah corrected. "Isn't it lovely? I love decorating for solstice."

"Yule," Reg repeated, looking around. "I thought Yule was Christmas? Yuletide greetings and all of that. Isn't that right?"

"Christians may think that Yule and Christmas are the same

things because they borrowed so many of the symbols and traditions from Yule, but they are not the same thing. This is for our holy day. Little Jesus couldn't have been born in December. Not if sheep were lambing in the fields."

"Uh… oh. Okay. I don't know much about the origins of either of them. I mean I've been forced to watch or read the Christmas story enough times, with all of the different foster families who wanted to educate me as to what Christmas was really about, but I never really saw the connection between a baby being born and Christmas and all of the rest—gifts and Santa Claus and…" She looked around, "…this."

"That's because there is no connection. It is a bunch of traditions cobbled together in an effort to keep the pagan converts happy hundreds of years ago. Christmas today is a chaotic mishmash of Christian legend and pagan symbolism and Coca Cola and Clement Clarke Moore. Hallmark and commercialism. Nothing like Yule." She folded her arms and looked around at the decorations adorning every surface with a contented smile. "I love the simple symbolism and stories of Yule. They have barely changed during the time that Christianity was trying to get a foothold and build its empire. Still the same symbols and rituals that have always been part of the season."

Reg indicated the garlands of twinkle lights. "Nothing has changed?"

"Well, if you want to bring modern technology into it. It is a little easier to string lights than it is to try to fill the house with candles. Most of these…" Sarah indicated one of the many candles flickering around the room, "are actually electric." She reached into one jar and pulled the fake candle out, not burning herself. "I get them at the dollar store by the case."

Reg laughed. "Well, you wouldn't want to burn the house down."

"Yule is a time of light, so I always try to provide lots of extra inspiration. You do want a few real candles to practice meditation and healing, but most of them can just be electric."

Reg picked up another of the fake candles and looked at it. She put it back down. "Healing?"

"Fire is a powerful element. It can hurt and do devastating damage, but it can also heal."

"I'll have to take your word on that one."

"If you want to learn about it, I am more than happy to share."

"Yeah… why don't you tell me about the rest? Are you telling me that the Christmas tree is really a Yule tree?"

"Yes, it is," Sarah laughed. "Evergreen trees and branches were a symbol of life for long before the Christians borrowed them. They stay green all winter with the promise of reawakening in the spring. How could that not be a powerful symbol in any pagan culture?"

"Well, I guess." Reg looked around. "Not that anything turns brown in December here. It's sort of funny to be somewhere green all year long."

"It is paradise," Sarah agreed. "I have had enough of cold nights, snow, mud, and miserable weather. Florida is the perfect place."

"As long as there are no hurricanes," Reg suggested.

"Well." Sarah shrugged, conceding the point. "I'd still rather be warm all year. My old bones do not like the cold."

Reg supposed that if Sarah were hundreds of years old, as she claimed, she was entitled to complain about aching bones.

"When is Yule? Is it the same day as Christmas?"

"It is winter solstice. December twenty-first. But it is traditionally held for twelve days, so—"

"The twelve days of Christmas?"

"You didn't ever wonder where that came from?"

"Uh… no."

Reg had always had more pressing concerns around Christmas time. Was she living in a home where she was expected to give gifts? That could be a problem, especially if it was supposed to be paid for out of her own money, something she rarely had.

Was she going to be staying with her foster family for Christmas, or would they be visiting extended family and she would be required to go to respite care for the holiday, where the parents would know nothing about her?

Would she be forced to sing? To perform? To sit through mind-numbing hours of preaching? Or would it be a family that didn't celebrate Christmas and was sneered at by the kids at school and other people in the neighborhood? Many years, she had wished that she could just skip Christmas. She had never once been tempted to research Christmas traditions and to find out where they had come from.

"I'll tell you more about it later, then. We have plenty of time. I wanted to get the decorations up early to get plenty of usage out of them. I'm not one to put them up the day before Yule and take them down again the day after."

"Sure, that makes sense. You may as well enjoy it all."

Sarah clearly did, or she wouldn't have been decorating the cottage as well as her own house. Reg assumed that it was not a Yule tradition to decorate other people's homes.

"Are you going to decorate the tree?"

"You and I can do that over the next few days. I'm afraid I'm out of energy today. The well has run dry."

"Okay." Reg might have fun decorating a tree. But she couldn't make any assumptions as to what they would be putting on it. She was pretty sure that round Christmas baubles and an angel on top of the tree would not be part of the prescribed decorations. "Well, thank you for all of this. It's lovely. I didn't expect anything. I thought when I came home, and the lights were on that... it might have been burgled."

Sarah laughed heartily. "No, just an old lady who doesn't know when to stop. I'm going to get something to eat and hit the sack. I will not be out partying tonight."

* * *

Delusions of the Past, Book #9 of the *Reg Rawlins, Psychic Investigator* series by P.D. Workman can be purchased at pdworkman.com

ABOUT THE AUTHOR

Award-winning and USA Today bestselling author P.D. (Pamela) Workman writes riveting mystery/suspense and young adult books dealing with mental illness, addiction, abuse, and other real-life issues. For as long as she can remember, the blank page has held an incredible allure and from a very young age she was trying to write her own books.

Workman wrote her first complete novel at the age of twelve and continued to write as a hobby for many years. She started publishing in 2013. She has won several literary awards from Library Services for Youth in Custody for her young adult fiction. She currently has over 60 published titles and can be found at pdworkman.com.

Born and raised in Alberta, Workman has been married for over 25 years and has one son.

* * *

Please visit P.D. Workman at pdworkman.com to see what else she is working on, to join her mailing list, and to link to her social networks.

* * *

If you enjoyed this book, please take the time to recommend it to other purchasers with a review or star rating and share it with your friends!

facebook.com/pdworkmanauthor

twitter.com/pdworkmanauthor

instagram.com/pdworkmanauthor

amazon.com/author/pdworkman

bookbub.com/authors/p-d-workman

goodreads.com/pdworkman

linkedin.com/in/pdworkman

pinterest.com/pdworkmanauthor

youtube.com/pdworkman